KEL BRUEM

What's Luck Got to Do With It

This book was professionally typeset on Reedsy.
Find out more at reedsy.com

For Guramar and Jack
Who fell in love in Boston

Contents

1

Caoimhe

Dan held the paper bag full of coffee beans against his chest, drumming his fingers along it and arching an eyebrow at me suggestively.

Come on, I thought to myself. *You're in the goddamn doorway, just a little further.*

"I had a great time," he purred.

"Yeah," I smiled.

"Next time, I'll make us coffee. In the morning. You know," he wiggled the arched eyebrow.

I held in a wince, keeping the smile plastered across my face. "Oh yeah?" I managed, my voice pitched up an octave—the register I reserved for pissed-off talent and clients.

Did you buy the beans at the cafe just so you could use that line?

"I'll text you tomorrow, Came," he leaned in for a kiss that I dodged by pretending to fiddle with the deadbolt lock.

"It's still Caoimhe," I said, still smiling, still obliging. You'd think by this point in my life I'd be used to fucking dudes who couldn't get my name right. If I made that the minimum requirement to sleep with me, there'd be cobwebs between my legs. And I was really only willing to tolerate one fire hazard at a time in my life.

"Right, sorry, your name…it's just so hard. I'm never gonna get it right," he said, still standing in my doorway, still petting the coffee beans. "Would it be ok if I called you C?"

"No," I winked at him. "Night, Dan."

I swung the door shut on his slightly startled face as he sputtered out, "Okay, talk soon!" through the rapidly closing space between us.

"No, the fuck we will not," I whispered to my now graciously empty apartment.

I only meant to meet Dan for the traditional App Date Coffee Scope Out—the part of any single person's dating life where they make sure strangers on the internet are who they say they are by meeting in real life.

I must've been hornier than I realized—it had been *a long time*—because after two or three giggles at Dan's barely funny jokes, I invited him back to my place.

Wandering into the kitchen, I pulled out a pot and my treasured steel-cut oats. We were tumbling into an early Boston fall, and the air had turned crisp as Dan and I walked to my apartment. I heaved a sigh and put water on to boil, measuring out the oats.

I thought it would be nice to have some human contact—a quick lay at best, a little snuggling on the couch at least. Dan was immediately into the former over the latter which was a huge letdown—except there was nothing huge about it.

I wondered if I should be nicer about this recurring theme in my love life. It's not anyone's fault I'm a size queen—I'd ditch the attitude if I could. It just seemed like *no one* was ever big enough. I'd figured out it was a side effect of my family's particular type of magic, one that I discovered around the same time I discovered boys. You can imagine why I didn't go running to Mom or Grandma to ask if they had the same problem, even though Grandma was always ready with rules and advice for a young leprechaun entering the world.

And it's not like I could call her up and ask if there was a way to control it. I got excited, and my vagina got greedy. *No one* wants to talk to their grandmother with a greedy vagina.

She'd be pissed to know I was bringing home human men anyway.

"You'll never be able to offer your real self to them, not without risking their violence and greed," she told me once. *"You're setting yourself up for disappointment."*

The pisser was she didn't even know the half of it.

I poured the oats in, stirred, and covered the pot.

"You've still got my back, though." I tapped the handle with affection, thinking about the immediate comfort a hot bowl of oats with just a little whiskey in it would bring after yet another cold toss in the sheets.

I went in search of my phone to set a timer. Pete would be *pissed* if I set off another fire alarm because I forgot my oatmeal again.

I checked my nightstand, ignoring how utterly undisturbed my bed looked despite having just had company. I checked under my nightstand, under the bed, and behind the headboard. There were only so many places it could be in my one-bedroom apartment and it wasn't like Dan had me throwing my things in a wild passionate rush to the bed.

If only.

When my phone wasn't in-between the couch cushions or in my purse, I knew something happened to it. I heaved yet another disappointed sigh and went to the jar I kept on top of the fridge. Pulling a thimble from amid the other sparkly debris and coins, I stomped to my balcony door, slamming it open. I set the thimble down on the wood slats, careful not to let it wobble through the cracks.

"You guys aren't funny!"

I turned around in the doorway, counted to five, and sure enough, a bell-like giggle chimed from where I left the offering.

When I turned back around, instead of my phone, there was a

minuscule naked woman with sparkling dragonfly wings holding the thimble.

Fucking fairies.

I knelt to bring the five-inch creature closer to my level.

"My phone?" I held my hand out, waiting.

The fairy considered my open palm with multi-faceted eyes. Sometimes, I thought they looked much more like bugs than Fae. It sent a chill down my back when I remembered we were related.

"I wonder what Dame Ryan would say if she knew about your latest guest," the fairy teased, studying the thimble closely.

"Probably that I should be a little more discerning if I don't want to keep being let down," I said. I meant it as a joke about Dan's tiny dick, but it rang true to my grandmother's sentiments about keeping human company.

"Sounds like you've had this conversation already," the fairy sighed, apparently bored. "I guess I'll have to tell her that—"

I reached out and snatched the fairy's left wing, pinching it carefully between my thumb and forefinger. She shrieked, a sound I was sure only Fae and dogs could hear.

"My phone," I said through gritted teeth.

"Mercy, mercy! Please, Duchess!"

I rolled my eyes and let go, but not before pinching a final time. I *hated* it when they used my title like that—like they knew it would make me remember who and what I am.

It did.

"I'm going to look away now so you can do what you must, but when I look again my phone better be where you're standing—and you better not be."

I turned my head until I couldn't see the fairy anymore and counted to five. The fairy giggled again, and I swear I heard her fart near my ear on her way out. When I turned back, sure enough, there was my phone.

I'd left the dating app open to my, *"Be right there,"* message to Dan. Sighing, I tapped my own profile to scan it for the thousandth time for hints that I was attracting bad bed karma. There was my smiling Fae-like face—freckles, wide hazel eyes, and a bewitching mouth.

Not being cute, I literally had those attributes. They were a charming byproduct of my human-size glamour. I couldn't squash all of my true self entirely just because I was essentially on the "extra-large" setting. It was also why I still had intensely blonde curly hair. "Strenuously curly" my best friend called it, because it looked like I did each wisp by hand every morning.

But that was magic for you. Always making things look impossibly good.

Or just impossible.

I flipped through the photos I'd posted—all smiling, approachable, friendly.

Normal.

Painfully normal.

"Maybe that's my problem," I whispered to myself. Maybe I was attracting small-dick energy because I wasn't putting out magic coochie vibes.

I suddenly remembered why I'd gone through all the trouble to get my phone in the first place when the familiar screech of the fire alarm in our building sounded.

"Fuuuuccckkkk," I sighed. I marched over to the stovetop where the oatmeal was crisped black in the pot. I punched the kitchen fan on, and ran for the back door again, setting the pot out where the smoke hopefully wouldn't waft back up to the smoke detectors.

But I wasn't fast enough.

Staccato knocking came from my front door. I swung it open to the downturned face of my stubby landlord, Pete.

"Old. Building. Miss Ryan." He emphasized each word by jabbing a dirty finger into his palm.

"I know, Pete, I'm so sorry it won't—"

"It *keeps* happening again, Miss Ryan."

The hairy mole on the right side of his face had gotten bigger since I last saw him—and hairier, if that was possible. It already looked like a grey patch of grass.

"Have we considered upgrading to detectors that aren't so sensitive?" It sounded stupid as soon as I said it.

"Yes, I'd love to make it easier to burn down a historic building because one of my tenants is a careless cook." He peered behind me into my living room like I was hiding a BBQ smoker and not an embarrassing pot of oats. "It would be cheaper to sign you up for cooking classes."

"Really?"

He rolled his eyes so hard I could see how yellowed the whites were.

"Hey good lookin', what's cookin'?" An unfamiliar voice called up the stairs and Pete revealed his yellows again. If he rolled his eyes any harder, they were going to wander off without him.

"Mr. Burleigh," Pete growled in what I guessed was a greeting.

A tall, built man with dark shoulder-length hair and attractive salt and pepper stubble rounded the staircase to the landing. He was carrying paper grocery bags in both arms, and they were heavy enough that I could see his biceps flexing underneath his jacket. He winked a startling grey eye at me, wiggling past Pete to stand just on the far side of the landing from us. He set down his groceries, pulling a set of keys from a carabiner on his belt loop.

"Mr. Burleigh is my father," he said. "You can call me Will."

"Will?" I hadn't met this man before but here he was acting as if he'd lived here for a decade. I racked my brain, trying to remember when Sandra across the hall moved out. Had I been so swallowed by work and my greedy vagina I hadn't noticed a new neighbor? My building was small enough I could usually at least recognize who lived there when we passed in the stairwell, but I prided myself on knowing everyone's names.

"Will, William, hell I'll even take a Bill here or there—so long as it's a Benjamin or a Jackson." He winked again—which was charming but did nothing to clarify what was happening in front of me.

"Mr. Burleigh is my newest tenant," Pete said, unphased by the wave of enthusiasm Will brought up the stairs with him.

"And a pretty good cook if I do say so," Will said, pushing open his door. "Did I hear talk of cooking lessons?"

"Miss Ryan burns everything she tries to feed herself."

I blushed, somewhere between humiliated and irritated. Will was handsome but I mostly just wanted to eat something and finish an episode of *Kissing Strange Men to Get Married*.

"A girl's gotta stay thin," I quipped.

"I think this girl's got a fine figure already," Will said, looking me up and down with no subtlety.

I was *not* blushing because of that. Definitely not.

"I'm going to leave now." Pete looked disgusted, more so than usual. "Expect a fee for disturbances, Miss Ryan."

I was about to screech about legality, but Will cut me off.

"I don't think that's necessary, Pete." He set his groceries down, leaning forward on his doorframe as if it were the only thing keeping him from launching across the landing. "Not when you've got expert emergency personnel across the way. I'm an expert at sniffing out trouble, don't you worry."

I wasn't entirely comforted by that.

Pete considered him for a moment then wagged a finger between the two of us.

"Fine, but if the alarm sounds again because of Miss Ryan, you'll *both* receive a fee for disturbances."

"Thank you, sir," Will threw him a haphazard salute and winked at me again. Was this going to be a regular greeting between us? Something prickled along the back of my neck and I wondered if I was better off taking my chances with grumpy old Pete.

Pete shuffled off down the stairs, back to his basement unit where he lurked until someone tried to use the laundry machine.

"Thanks," I said. "And nice to meet you." I was about to shut my door, but Will's voice stopped me.

"We haven't, though," he said. "I don't know the fair maiden's name."

"Caoimhe," I said, barely hesitating. I waited for the knit brows, the squint, the attempted repetition.

Will grinned wide, revealing large teeth. There was something predatory in it and I felt a chill down my spine. *He's just a neighbor. We'll probably never see each other anyway.*

"A name from the old country," he said.

There again was the warning along my nerves. I shook it off and stifled a sigh.

"My folks were old school," I said. "Anyway, I still haven't eaten so…" I nodded toward my apartment and put a hand on the edge of my door. "Thanks again. I'm here if you need anything—a cup of sugar, burnt oatmeal."

A sharp-toothed smile. "I'll be sure to take you up on that."

2

Leith

As soon as the asshole's body hit the water, I knew there was no going back.

I let the worst of myself win—just like she always said I eventually would. I could hear her voice in my head, taunting me.

"You love those mortals but wait until they learn about your true nature. Wait until they see you've got teeth."

I'd stormed away from her that day, slamming out into a summer thunderstorm and never looked back. I thought I could prove her wrong. I thought if I kept a low profile, stayed hidden among the humans, they'd never know who I truly was. I could have the best of both worlds—the wonder and chaos of living in a mortal city next to the wild, insatiable call of the sea that sang in my very bones.

I was even happy for a minute.

Stupid to think running away would set me free from her.

Now, here it was, three months later, standing on the prow of my boat out on the Boston Harbor, staring down into the water at what I'd just done.

The man's blond head bobbed back up from under the water as he flailed his arms against the waves. His windbreaker worked against his strokes, weighing him down. There alongside his struggle was my own reflection—dark, tangled hair, grey eyes, mouth set in a firm line.

"You son of a bitch!" He screamed, just as Will came slamming up to the front of the boat next to me, flinging a life preserver out into the water.

"Great, Leith," Will hissed, pulling the rope taut and bringing the man closer to the side of the boat. "Really fucking great."

He stormed off to pull the man out of the water with the help of a few other passengers as I stared dumbfounded after him.

And then I realized forty pairs of eyes were staring at me. I turned to see every passenger on the Mister Flipper looking at me as if I was a monster.

They had no idea.

***

"What tinned fish do you have clunking around in your head that made you think that kind of behavior was okay?" Kelly wasn't screaming. Kelly never screamed. But when Kelly's face got red and her voice got low, a finely honed edge slicing the air with every word, she didn't need to scream.

"Kel, I—"

"Do not," she hissed, "hit me with a sweet apology. The reputation of our entire company depended on that ride going well, Leith. You may as well have thrown me in with that jackass."

"See! He—"

"Everyone agrees he was out of line, Leith," Will chimed in from where he was sitting in the far corner, blowing cigarette smoke out the open window. We were in the Mister Flipper office, a cramped, sun-bleached room coated in a thick layer of dust. The walls were covered in framed Polaroids of Kelly and Will from their early days together, starting the company and exploring Boston as two unusual creatures in the human world. Kelly stood behind her desk, scowling

10

at us over stacks of business school textbooks, boat manuals, and what I assumed was miscellaneous paperwork that probably needed filing with the city.

"You're the one driving the boat." Kelly pushed black curls out of her face and looked at her phone screen for the thousandth time since I walked in the office. Her long nails seemed to stretch in the shadows of the office, hinting at her true form. Not that Kelly tried to hide it. Most humans saw a female siren and simply thought they were passing by another attractive, fashionable woman.

"You have to keep your cool," she continued. "You have to lead by example when you have forty-five people out on the water. And you have to provide the best possible *unique* experience for the people paying to take our tours or we'll fade into the background of all the other options—especially when we have investors onboard."

"Kel I am not—"

"I'm not saying you have to jump in," she threw her hands in the air and then leveled them at me like an air traffic controller.

"But look at you." She waved her hands up and down. "You're a fucking smoke show with those strong boatman arms, soulful eyes, stupid artist hair. You could have our queue filled every morning with horny moms and grandmas trying to get an eyeful of a fantasy for an hour before going back to their lazy husbands."

Will coughed on his cigarette then immediately started cackling.

"You too, Dick Wasty," she snapped. "You could both be taking turns playing the cool brooding seaman with his charming roguish co-captain and we'd just be raking it in."

I didn't know where to look, overwhelmed by Kel's long list of compliments.

"But *no*, you have to throw a temper tantrum when someone looks at you sideways," she pointed a threatening finger at me before leveling it at Will. "And you can't stay sober long enough to catch the bus much less your own boat."

"Hey, I was there today," Will stubbed out his cigarette in indignation.

Kelly arched an eyebrow and slow clapped for a few moments. Will had the decency not to flinch.

"Today," she said. "Perfect. You were there, *today*."

Her phone pinged and she threw her head back to the ceiling. Will and I both clamped hands over our ears instinctively, but she was too distracted by the notification to notice. Thankfully, she didn't scream. But that didn't stop her from swearing.

"Fuck fuck fuckity shit." She held up the screen, where a looped video of me throwing the man into the harbor had been shared. I wasn't sure what the site was, but I knew a number that high couldn't be good.

"Already?" Will was next to me now, peering at the screen.

"No one has to format the footage from VHS anymore, you Luddite. Of course, it's already up." Kelly put the phone down and pinched the bridge of her nose.

"Leith, go home. Will, you're solo the rest of the day—*if* anyone even shows up."

"You can't punish me for his bullshit!" Will protested.

"The fuck I can't. You convinced me to hire him. You better hope people arrive for the two thirty and four o'clock tours or you're going to be scraping barnacles with a toothpick for the rest of the day."

We both stared. Kelly had gotten mad before, but she never sent anyone home and she definitely *never* threatened Will with barnacle duty. He was her golden captain. They'd started Mister Flipper together and she always treated him more like a partner than an employee.

"Now," she said her voice like a whisper through reeds. We bumped into each other trying to fit through the door at the same time.

"I thought sirens were supposed to be charming," Will muttered, putting another cigarette between his teeth.

"Shut up." I nudged him and glanced back at the closed office door behind us.

"She doesn't scare me." He puffed up his chest and squinted over my shoulder like a hero in a western movie.

"You nearly took me out trying to get to the door first."

"Trying to be respectful of a lady's need to screech," he said, exhaling a cloud of smoke. "What're you gonna do with the rest of your day?"

I shrugged. I wasn't looking forward to the yawning openness of what should've been a busy workday. I could already feel the guilt and shame bubbling up in my stomach over my actions.

"Feel sorry for yourself?"

I rolled my eyes. Will knew me like a brother, which gave his teasing a sharper edge than I enjoyed.

"You need new hobbies." Will threw me a wave over his shoulder as he headed back toward the dock. I refused to let him have the last word, so I picked the first afternoon activity I could think of.

"A museum!" I called back to him, knowing my response was too late and he probably couldn't hear me.

"Wow!" He hollered back and I could see his shoulders shaking in laughter.

3

Leith

The Museum of Fine Arts never ceased to make me marvel at human ingenuity. The sweeping marble entrance, the rotunda in the center, the way each painting pulled you forward to the next one until suddenly you were lost in the heart of the building, unsure even what year it was.

I loved it.

After leaving the docks, I wandered into an exhibit filled with rural scenes—meadows, mountains, forests, but also rivers and beaches and docks overlooking the sea. A plaque near the door told me these artists had taken their supplies with them and painted the location exactly as it was in that moment, aiming to capture the subtleties of light and color that would certainly be different the next time they were there.

A painting of a beach stopped me for a long time. I rarely let myself be rushed through a gallery, but today in particular, I felt a longing rise in my chest. The waves were capped in white as they made their way to the shore, and I could practically hear the call of the open ocean there in that museum, surrounded by security cameras and wood floors.

It was probably time to go for a swim.

I wandered through the rest of the exhibit, gazing at each different scene as the memory of my last swim washed over me.

I'd been with Jolie, a fellow mershark in town for a weekend visit and a friend of Will's. She called and asked if I'd join her since Will ditched her to chase a pretty girl through the Boston club scene that night.

It'd been a clear night as I stood on the pier, with a mostly full moon hanging heavy above us. Jolie leapt in naturally—no hesitation—but when she bobbed back up to the surface, teeth already sharpening in her face, she complained about the chill. I smiled to myself, smug over how tender tropical colleagues could be about the New England water.

I jumped in and here in the memory I always had to stop myself, had to get a grip on where I was and who was around me so I didn't immediately turn around and dash for the water as fast as I could.

The waves received me like a lover returning from a journey, open, eager, joyous. I'd felt it trilling along my spine even as the shift began, pounding adrenaline through my veins, a single word whispered again and again in my whole being.

Home.

Jolie went home after her visit, and since Will refused to get back into the water, her departure left a bigger hole than I expected. Busy summer waters at the harbor meant it hadn't been easy for me to take a swim in my true form for several months. Rather than risk ending up on someone's phone as a viral video, I decided to wait for the tourist crowds to clear out before giving in to a long swim in the fall. Maybe I'd try following the coast for a while, take a vacation from the tours for a week or so.

Too late, I realized my caution was for nothing—I ended up a viral video and I looked completely human while doing so.

Hot shame flooded my cheeks, and I rubbed a hand down my face trying to soothe myself.

Suddenly, not even art could help me feel better. I decided to cut this visit short, tucking the exhibit pamphlet into my back pocket and stepping out into the late afternoon sunshine.

Compared to the wildness of the sea I dreamed of, Boston's repetitious European architecture hit me like a stack of bricks. The rows of buildings—formerly housing for Brits in the New World—were identical, arching out to reach the horizon in each direction. Without the occasional garden plot or flag, I would've thought it was the same building.

I decided to stretch my legs, hoping for a distraction, but I barely made it past the park across the way before a frustrated itching burned under my skin. I didn't want to walk.

I let myself wander closer and closer to the water. The Charles River's saltwater joining at the harbor was mere steps away. No one would notice one weird man jumping in. It didn't matter even if they did.

I'd be long gone before anyone could arrive on the scene.

I passed the stately Victorian-era buildings that were mostly offices and an optometry school before stopping just within the line of trees that bordered the Charles River. The hum in my bones was more than a suggestion now. It was a demand so strong I felt like I would vibrate until I broke into pieces.

It would be quick.

No one would see.

This part of the river even had a dock.

I walked to the end of it, looking around nonchalantly for passersby. Given the sunny weather and light crisp in the air, the pathway was busy with joggers and dogwalkers.

I wouldn't have time to strip then. The next lull in pedestrian traffic might be the only one I would get.

When it came, I didn't hesitate, taking a single step off the dock and dropping down into the water at a straight angle.

Relief flooded my system immediately. The itching under my skin eased, the vibration in my bones quelled, the ache in my soul quieted.

For those few moments under the water, it was worth the risk of being seen.

The shift began and my heart soared at the promise of hours in the water unbothered as my legs fused into a strong tail, tearing through my clothes. My dorsal popped with a satisfying release of pressure along my spine and I realized Kelly would be pissed that I shredded another work polo.

I looked down at my now-webbed hands, the familiar speckled pattern spreading down my arms, and I took a deep breath with my gills.

It was as if I hadn't truly breathed since the summer. Everything in my body aligned, stilled, listened. The ceaseless current pulled and pushed, pulled and pushed, swirling the light above me in refracted patterns. I let myself sink further, knowing a shark fin above the waterline would attract attention.

Following the smell of salt in the water, the delicate shifting in temperature as the river opened up the ocean, I set off.

In the water, in my true form, nothing mattered but my basest instincts. I let my busy human mind settle into the background. The water was alive around me, thousands of microscopic critters chirping and singing to one another. If I were an actual whale shark, I would've followed their cries, dropping open my jaw to filter feed. It would be an automatic action, not something requiring hunting or attacking like my sharp-toothed cousins.

There she was again, flashing through my mind.

"Wait until they learn you have teeth."

I wriggled in the water, shaking the thought out into the current, and letting it drift away from me as I reached the mouth of the river. I wasted no time plunging directly into the shifting water, feeling the sudden expanse of the ocean clutch my heart and pull. I could've given in to that instinct, following it wherever my ancestors would've gone this time of year. I could've slipped away from my life in Boston, from

Kelly and Will, from Mister Flipper.

There weren't any investors to impress in the open ocean. No one cared if you lost your temper.

I closed my eyes and drifted in the open water for a moment as the day washed back over me, refusing to be lost to the tide.

The man, a potential investor who Kelly invited aboard with his family, was sitting in the sun with his daughter. She held up a pocket-sized sketch pad with a drawing of a mermaid on it.

"I hope we see a mermaid today, Daddy," she said, soft face filled with hope.

"Impossible," he'd said without even looking at her. "They're not real."

It was automatic—my fists, his jacket, and then the heft of hauling him over the side. The satisfaction of listening to him drop into the water before the reality of what I'd done set in.

I still don't know why I lost it like that. Maybe I was wound up from not having been in the water in months. Maybe it was the broken look on the little girl's face—a potential artist squashed before she could even start. Whatever the trigger, I'd already messed up, and I'd let down the two most important people in my life in the process.

I'd landed in Boston on accident, following a band on tour from New Orleans that had beguiled me from the water in the first place then lured me across the country with their all-too-human music. We were at an after party for the band when Will recognized me for what I was from across the room, parting the crowd like a predator through the water to reach me. I hadn't known how desperately I needed to be seen until he clapped a hand on my shoulder, his trademark grin splitting his face. Kelly had given me a place to belong when I had nowhere else, welcoming me onto the team with no questions asked.

I'd repaid them both with massive and potential losses to their livelihood—to *our* livelihood.

I thought again of the paintings on land—the captured light, the emotion in a single frozen glance.

I swam back toward the harbor.

I wouldn't follow the ocean's call just yet.

***

Kelly's office was dark and empty, although it was barely six o'clock. There was a peculiar window that ran along the floor, just wide enough to fit the shoulders of a man through. Will had pointed it out to me when I started, nonchalantly noting that Kelly also kept spare uniforms in the office closet for anyone who might get a little too damp during their shift.

It was work, shimmying up the dock support then hauling myself through the window while naked. If I got splinters in my balls, I was going to make Will pluck them out as payment for even suggesting this route. Couldn't we get a ladder if two mersharks worked at the same place?

I flopped on the floor, exhausted—from the day, the swim, the climb. But I barely had time to catch my breath when I heard the office door open and close.

I froze, unsure if I should move to cover myself and risk drawing the incomer's attention, or just stay as still as possible.

Heavy footsteps sounded across the wooden floor, and I held my breath as they grew closer. It wasn't a large office—I had nowhere to go, and they didn't have far.

Will's grinning face leaned over me, teeth sharp and bright in the dark.

"Just the man I wanted to see."

I let out my breath in a whoosh, rustling Will's long dark hair across his face. He scowled and waved the air in front of him.

"Ugh, you smell like plankton."

I sat up and went to the closet, quickly hauling on a pair of pants and a hoodie.

"You know I don't feed," I said.

"Yeah, but it's still fun to tease you about it."

"Where's Kelly?" I nodded to the vacant desk.

"She left after I set off with the four p.m. Said she needed a drink and a think."

"So do I." I rummaged through the bottom of the thin closet looking for something that could pass for shoes, but no luck.

"Try the cabinet, one over," Will said around a fresh cigarette. I smelled it as the flame caught, grateful for the worn sneakers I found in the first drawer. They could've been stilettos and I would've put them on to get out of sitting in a smoke-filled room with Will.

"I don't know how you tolerate that shit," I said as I struggled into the shoes. They were maybe a size too small.

"It's been longer for me," he said, exhaling as I reached for the door. "I'm not as sensitive anymore."

"I wouldn't be either if I killed my senses off on purpose." As soon as I said it, I knew it was too much—especially after today.

"Hey, buddy," Will leaned in the doorway of the office, watching me with a predator's focus. "I don't tell you how to live your life, even though watching you mope around this place is so fucking depressing. So maybe mind your own seabed before trying to root around in mine."

I looked away, letting him win the stare down. Because I was tired. Because my heart ached with something I couldn't name.

But not because he was right.

Will smoked and drank himself into a stupor and it was all because he wouldn't shift into his true form. His shark senses were screaming at him to get back into the water—just once—and he wouldn't do it. He'd rather kill himself slowly.

"I'll mind my business when you learn to share yours," I said, unsure if I really wanted him to hear me.

"Alright, alright," Will held his hands up in the air, but the tension was not gone from his shoulders and his voice was sharp. "I thought we could have a beer and blow off some steam together. Maybe get the jitters out before you're back tomorrow and all nervous about pissing off our great Mistress."

I hated when he did this but there was no stopping the defensive sarcasm once it started.

"But I can see we're deep in brooding artist mode for the evening, so I will allow the gentleman to stew as he sees fit." Will bowed with a flourish before slamming the office door shut behind me.

Great. Now he really would be too drunk tomorrow to catch a bus.

I squared my shoulders and tried to let it go, letting the city lights swallow me on my way home, leaving the dark call of the ocean behind.

4

Caoimhe

By the time my meeting with a new client ended and we'd shaken hands, sparking our soon-to-be working relationship, I'd missed six calls from my grandmother.

Fucking fairies.

"Thank you again, Caoimhe," he said, sounding out my name slowly but surely. He was a singer with gold eyes and a sideways smile. I'd listened to his debut album and nearly fallen in love myself. Unfortunately, he'd been trying to book shows with a lullaby and his Instagram was filled with pictures of sunsets and sunflowers. Eve had sent him my way, like she usually did, when his press release came across her desk at The World.

"You're welcome, Darren," I said. "I'll email you the contract by the end of this week and we can get going. I can't wait." He flashed me that shy smile again as we both left the cafe.

I headed back to my own apartment, knowing that I was due for yet another lecture—one that I definitely shouldn't try to take on the street.

The late afternoon sunlight was warm on the surrounding brick buildings, giving the street a rosy glow. The cobblestones beneath me created a familiar uneven tip-toed dance and every time I made it to the corner without tripping it felt like reassurance that I'd found my home.

If only I could get my family to let me settle in completely.

I jiggled my key in the front door to the building, holding its wooden weight against my hip as I reached in for the second front door, which was considerably older and much less weather-proofed than its creaky cousin.

I knew my grandmother was going to want to know why I insisted on staying in a mortal city, why I wouldn't come home and claim my title, and why I kept dallying with human men. I could hear her in my head going on about wasted time and prospects. She'd be livid that another member of the Fae had seen me and was probably spreading it around to any creature with ears.

The stairs to my apartment were carpeted wood, with a thick banister rubbed dull by hundreds of hands over time. The carpet was plush, though the pattern had faded, and it dampened the sound of thudding footsteps as we all moved about our daily lives. There was a single window above the first curve of the stairs with stained glass leaves intertwining across the frame, sending green and yellow light flitting across the entryway. A heavy wooden cabinet stood directly to the right of the door, piled high with newspapers, weeklies, and notices for community markets on the various college campuses across the city.

Not for the first time, I wondered how I would explain to my grandmother that the answer to all her demands was that I'd found a home—one I wasn't going to give up.

Upstairs, I opened my windows to let in the crisp air and pulled a beer from the fridge. It was maybe a little early in the day, but I wasn't going to have this conversation unfortified.

I took a deep breath and tapped the "return call" button.

It rang once before my grandmother's voice came shrill through the speaker.

"I see Her Royal Highness has deigned to return my call." She had the thick Irish accent my parents had worked so hard to blend out of their own voices when they moved to the states so many decades ago.

"You've told me before, Nan, a Duchess doesn't get to be referred to as Her Highness," I shot back, using the familial nickname I knew she hated.

She clicked her teeth, and I could hear her adjusting the phone, then the faint clink of ice in a glass. So, I wasn't drinking alone.

"You know why I'm calling, then?"

I nodded, then said, "I assume you heard from your latest spy."

"What our fairy cousins get up to on their excursions to the States is none of my business until it concerns my granddaughter playing with fire."

I thought of Dan's lukewarm kisses and cold hands. "I think fire is a bit of an exaggeration."

"Caoimhe," she sighed. "You know you must stop this. You're going to be discovered and then you'll see how greedy those men can be."

I sipped my beer, knowing what came next.

"Humans think our kind are money machines, gold depositories. They think we know where the riches are and if we tell them we don't, then we're just hiding it for ourselves."

I let the rehearsed silence stretch between us for a few moments. Next, my grandmother would guilt me about the family lands awaiting my return, how they needed a Ryan's luck to flourish, how so few of our kind were left in the world these days and I should be with my community.

But instead, my grandmother let loose a rogue warhead I didn't know was in her arsenal.

"I can't bear to lose another member of our family the way we lost your father."

I slammed my beer down on the counter, watching the foam spew out the top from the force.

"That's not fair," I said. "You know that's not fair."

"It's true, Caoimhe," she said. "And I'm sorry for it."

"You're not," I spat. "You're just lonely and bitter. No wonder Mom refuses to come back."

I hated the words as they hung in the air, suspended by my rage. I hated that she twisted them out of me.

"If that's how you really feel," she said. Her voice was soft, wounded.

The line went silent, and I looked down at my phone to see she'd hung up.

I immediately knew who and what I needed. I tapped the screen a few times, then waited for the answer.

"Hey," I said. "It's me. I need you."

***

The bass vibrated up through the floor and into my chest, slamming in time to the heavy beat. The dance floor was packed, a writhing nest of bodies under flashing lights, sweating out the day's stressors.

Eve and I danced together, somewhere in the middle. Her eyes were closed, arms thrown up over her head, a soft smile spread across her face. I was holding both our drinks carefully, moving my hips and head in time. Eve opened her eyes and grinned at me, holding her hands out for our drinks.

"Your turn," she mouthed.

Eve and I had grown up in separate parts of the world, both obsessed with '90s vampire movies. There was always a slow pan shot of some hot goth girl gyrating to techno, perfect hair and makeup despite the sweat glistening on her shoulders. She'd put her hands above her head as she danced, clearly meant to look seductive. But Eve and I both agreed we thought those girls looked free. We called it Hot Vamp Time and it was what we did together when we needed to shake off something particularly shitty.

I gave Eve our drinks and closed my eyes, letting my body move to the music. But my moment was cut short when someone slammed into me. I looked up to see Eve, both drinks knocked to the floor, screaming at some dude bro over the music. I hooked an arm through hers, hauling her away before a fight broke out. I wasn't surprised to see the relief on the guy's face—Evelyn Sharp was not a woman to be fucked with.

Outside on the street, I stretched my arms out to welcome the fresh air, relishing the wave of goosebumps across my shoulders.

"I'm sorry, C," Eve said, rifling through her purse.

I shrugged, taking my jacket from her and grabbing her hand. "We both know that's why Hot Vamp Time can't happen solo in the real world. Too many dudes getting in the way of the camera operator."

She shook her head, running her hands through her spiky short hair like she was trying to ventilate her brain in the cold. I watched as she adjusted her makeup, wiping away flaked mascara without a smudge and fixing her lipstick without a mirror before unceremoniously dropping the tube back into the carnage of her bag. I was surprised she found it so quickly in the first place—Eve's bags were a mythic place unto themselves, and I often wondered if there wasn't some magic to their endless depths.

Eve was definitely human, confirmed by her ability to walk in the sun, ignore shiny objects on the ground, and touch iron with her bare hands. But I still clung to a small thread of hope that I wasn't hiding alone, that someday Eve would reveal a tail, or a small set of nubby horns and we could commiserate on a whole new level.

Not that my friendship with Eve wasn't enough as it was.

"So, what's left on the Shit Day Checklist," she asked, holding up her fingers as she listed. "We had fancy French food, bougie themed cocktails, and Hot Vamp Time."

"That only leaves…" I let the expectation build by trailing off, looking to Eve with a smile.

"Ice cream!" We both shrieked, ignoring a grimacing group of college bros flanking the sidewalk as we walked by.

"We should do a pint from the corner and put on *My Light, My Blood*," Eve said, walking faster toward the neon-lit promised land that was Joe's Food and Liquor near my building.

"Eve, come on, no," I whined. She *loved* the moody camp of the 2000s vampire romance movies. I couldn't bear it, even in an ironic way.

"Someday you'll learn to appreciate genius pastiche."

"Someday you'll admit your love for Bobby Robertson."

"Oh, I admit it," she said, sliding into her denim jacket as we neared Joe's. We'd cooled off from the club and the night was crisp around us. "It's my boy Bobby who won't write me back."

I stopped on the corner when we got to Joe's, when I saw a dejected but familiar figure smoking just outside.

"I'll take my usual," I told Eve. "Give me one second."

My new neighbor was leaning against the brick wall, the outside lights under the canopy harsh across his face. A fresh pack of cigarettes was open in his hand, and I smelled cheap liquor as I got closer.

"Will, right?" I asked. He swayed heavily, turning his entire body so he could focus on me. I saw then he was holding an empty bottle of something. The charm was gone from his eyes, replaced with such a hollowness I felt my heart break on the spot.

"'Sup," he said, popping his lips on the "p."

"Oh boy," I sighed. "Come on, dude." I pulled the empty bottle from his hand, which he let slide loose with no complaint, and took him by the arm.

Eve stepped out with the dessert goods and arched both her eyebrows at me. "Who's your friend?"

"Will," I said. "He's pretty messed up. Getting him home safe is on the way."

"You're pretty," Will pointed toward Eve, missing her by about a foot.

"No, you are," Eve shot back, grinning despite herself.

"Eve," I warned.

"He did this to himself, C. I'm not gonna be sorry for him."

"She's right," Will agreed, nodding solemnly. He stopped a moment, turned in a circle, swayed, and then let me lead him to our two-pronged front door. He swayed in place while I fumbled out my keys to the outer door, quickly pulling it open and repeating the process with the inner door. I shoved Will through as Eve followed us.

"You're gonna drag him up the stairs?" Eve was skeptical.

"Carry me, mommy!" Will threw his arms around me, reeking of cigarettes and sweat. But there was something else underneath, something briny.

I pushed him off, but not hard enough to knock him over.

"You smell like a fucking shrimp boat," I said. "Carry yourself."

"It's a tour boat, thank you," he said in a prim tone, looking down his nose at me and Eve from the first few stairs. "Best harbor tour this city's ever seen, if Leith doesn't drown anyone else."

I gave him a nudge on the back to keep going. It would take us the rest of the night to get up one floor at this rate.

"Oh fun, your new neighbor is friends with a murderer," Eve quipped.

"'Snot a killer, he's a s'whale snark."

I sighed and turned around to Eve, mouthing "stop" as she slammed a hand over her mouth, eyes crinkling in laughter. I gave Will another nudge and we finally reached our landing.

"Alright, where are your keys?" I held my hand out for his house key.

"Don't have one," he said, blinking at me dumbly.

"It's your apartment, Will, you have a key. I saw you use it yesterday."

He shrugged, holding his empty hands out. Then he jumped, grabbing his ass with a giggle.

Eve's hand reached around from behind him where she still stood on the stairs, the landing not large enough to hold all three of us. She jingled Will's carabiner of keys tauntingly.

"I like her," Will whispered to me loudly.

"Yeah, me too."

Will's apartment was dark, still half-full of boxes. But his couch was cleared, thank god, and I guided him to it, letting him slump over.

"Drink some water," I said, turning to go, but he caught my hand.

"We're fucked," he said, and there was the sadness, surfacing up to still his lively presence. "We can't take the hit to our reputation. Kelly will never…" His voice trailed off into a soft sob. I looked over to see Eve's silhouette in the doorway. I nodded to her that I was okay and sat down on the couch next to Will.

"Did something happen today?" I asked.

He nodded. "Stupid Leith. You'd think a whale shark…" his voice trailed off as he looked up at me from under shaggy brown hair. "We need the world's greatest spin doctor."

"Well, I can't help with that. I'm not exactly—"

"No," he interrupted, shaking his head. "You're something else, aren't you? I can tell."

I wiggled my hand free from Will's grasp, my blood running cold. I remembered the predatory bite in his smile the day before and decided it was time to go.

"Maybe take some aspirin when you drink that water," I said, standing up and walking to the door where Eve was waiting.

"Hey, Caoimhe," he called. I turned to see him laid flat on the couch, feet poking over the arms. He waved a hand above the back of the couch and gave me a thumbs up. "Thanks."

"Good night, Will."

I locked the knob and closed the door behind me, shoving Eve onto the landing and toward my own front door.

"C, what the actual—"

"Shhhhh." My heart was pounding, and I desperately needed more than one closed door between me and Will.

It wasn't until I turned the dead bolt peeled off my club clothes and joined Eve on the couch finally that I felt my panic subsiding.

You're something else, aren't you?

He was just another big-city drunk weirdo. He hadn't meant anything by it.

"So, your hot neighbor is into you," Eve said around the spoon in her mouth, one hand holding the remote where she'd paused the opening scene of *My Light, My Blood*. Clearly, I already lost this vote.

"You always do this," I sighed, wiggling happily into the blanket across our laps, my pajamas soft against my freshly cleaned skin. "Just because a drunk man talks to me does not mean he's into me."

"He called you 'something else,'" Eve pressed. "Last I checked that was a pretty big compliment."

"He called you pretty," I countered, leveling my spoon at her seriously. "*And* he said he liked you, point blank."

Eve rolled her eyes, then threw me a mock snarl. "God, Caoimhe, stop trying to steal my boyfriend."

She clicked the remote at the TV and I relaxed into the comfort of a familiar end to the night.

5

Caoimhe

Loud knocking woke me up the following morning. My entire body was stiff from sleeping weird on the couch—and shoving my hefty neighbor up the stairs.

You're something else, aren't you?

I stretched against the pain in my neck, shoving aside Eve's feet from where they were tucked near my face. The knocking persisted, louder and more frantic.

"Hold on, god," I called, shuffling to the door.

Soft light trickled across the tops of the buildings around us, and I heard faint bird chirping. It had to be nearly seven a.m.

I flung open the door about to destroy whoever had the gall to—

"You're a publicist." Will was miraculously freshly showered and shaved. His hair was neatly combed back from his face revealing sharper features than I'd initially noticed. He was wearing a pressed polo with a boat insignia on the right shoulder and well-fitted Dickies. He looked like an entirely different person, all traces of the hollowed man from the night before erased.

"You're a publicist, right?" He repeated, barely giving me time to register what was happening. I nodded, dumbly.

"I have a job for you," he said. "We'll pay, whatever your rate. Say you can start today."

"How did you—"

"Pete told me, just now, when I was downstairs trying to mind my own business and get my work uniform from the dryer."

"He's too cute to be a stalker," Eve called from behind me, her voice rough with sleep.

To his credit, Will's gaze didn't so much as flicker away from my face, eyes pleading.

I shook my head—to clear it and in answer. "I'm not taking new clients right now," I said. "I'm sorry."

"You have to take this one."

"Will," I sighed. "It is early. There is no coffee. And I don't like being told what to do."

"Caoimhe." He took my hands in his and I was surprised at the gentleness with which his calloused skin brushed mine. "I would consider it a neighborly favor if you would at least come and hear us out."

"She'll do it," Eve breathed from over my shoulder. I flinched at her sudden appearance but neither she nor Will stirred, finally locking eyes as if I wasn't there.

I wiggled my hands free from Will's to put them on my hips.

"Who is 'we?'"

"Mister Flipper," he answered without breaking his staring contest with Eve.

"Answer's still no," I said. "Even if I were taking new clients, I don't do companies. Just individuals."

A musical chime came from Will's pocket, and he broke his trance-like gaze with Eve, leaping onto the first stair.

"I have to go prove all my coworkers wrong," he said. He grinned up at us, back to his sharp-toothed self. "Come to the Harbor today."

"No, I have work to do," I called down the stairs after him.

"Yeah! I know!" He called back from the ground floor. The stairs shuddered as he shut the front door behind him.

I turned to Eve, crossing my arms and arching an eyebrow. She was flushed, mouth dropped open like she'd seen something wondrous.

"You're impossible." I closed the door, snapping my best friend back to real life.

"You're going," she said, rushing across my apartment to the bathroom.

"Oh, are you my manager now?"

"You're going because I'm going with you and your neighbor is too hot to ignore."

"Don't you have to work?"

I watched as she flung her PJs across the hall into my bedroom, poking her head out the mostly closed bathroom door.

"Yeah, at nine. That's why we're going now." She shut the door and ran the clattering shower, drowning my protests with the groans of old pipes.

There was not enough coffee in this realm or any others.

***

The sky held the threat of rain as we climbed up and out from the T station. I checked my phone for the thousandth time, disliking this frantic disruption to my normal weekday routine. I had a client call at nine-thirty which would require a lengthy pep-talk before the writer's debut reading later that night. I didn't want to be frazzled from giving the "it's not you it's me" refusal to potentially an entire boat crew.

But Eve had my free hand in a death grip and was dragging me toward the docks like they might disappear with the sunrise.

"You *did* see him too drunk to walk last night, right?" I asked for maybe the thousandth time.

"You *did* see his eyes, right?" She shot back. Each time she had a different feature or turn of phrase he'd said off-handedly that had somehow become burned into the Horny Center of her brain. "We all have rough nights. I'm not writing off Hot Sailor Neighbor for it."

"Tour boat operator," I corrected trying not to roll my eyes straight out of my head.

A tell-tale tinkling bell came from somewhere directly above us. Eve didn't seem to notice, continuing her sled-dog pull on my arm. But I heaved a massive sigh and glanced up.

Fucking fairies.

"That's exactly what I need right now," I muttered.

"Shut up, we're here!" Eve squealed before dropping my hand to adjust her outfit. Despite having slept on my couch after drinking and dancing, her "morning after" look was effortless—a slouchy graphic printed t-shirt paired with neutral bike shorts and a fanny pack slung over her chest. Her thin sunglasses and light dusting of makeup made her look like someone's cool aunt out running errands, as if the suggestion of a more fashionable wardrobe not immediately within sight made the rest of her clothes still passable for exciting.

It was her own personal magic.

If I showed up in a big T and bike shorts, I'd look like a slob who escaped from the basement.

I didn't have to meet any *current* clients in person until after lunch, so I'd opted for a t-shirt and jeans, hair clipped up against the harbor's wind.

"The cavalry has arrived!" Will trumpeted from down the docks, waving his arms wide in the air.

"Be cool," Eve said to me from the side of her mouth while simultaneously pumping her arms in the air to return Will's greeting.

I followed her reluctantly onto the creaking wood boards, trying to keep my breathing steady, listening to the slosh of the waves against the support beams.

I *hated* having to decline a client—especially when I knew what I could do for them.

There was the usual desire not to let anyone down, to be as helpful as I could for people who had something beautiful to give to this world. If I didn't believe everyone had their own unique art to offer—art that mattered, that had power—I wouldn't be in this business. It always broke my heart to have to say no when I was already overbooked. I'd wonder for days after whose life I had left unchanged by that artist or that songwriter. What tough time would be ten times tougher without the novel I'd just walked away from?

But then there was my family's gift.

Without the Ryan lands to tend, to pour my ancestral luck and charm into, I found my powers manifesting at work. My clients *always* got their big break with me—sometimes even as early as their first event, first debut, first gig. I just had to show up and luck did the rest.

Mister Flipper with a damaged reputation right at the tail end of summer was in desperate need of luck. And I was going to deny them.

It shifted the balance too much to grant my luck to actual companies instead of individuals—to people with full marketing departments and budgets to throw at good PR. I decided early on that I'd only work with those who didn't have a clue about anything other than their art.

"Glad you came," Will said as we got closer. "Welcome to Mister Flipper. Let me take you to our fearless leader."

Eve hooked an arm through his, leaning into Will and grinning. "You make it sound like you're all from another planet."

Will winked. "Almost, ma'am. But there won't be probing until I take you to dinner."

"A true gentleman!" Eve giggled and let him lead her down the dock toward a rickety-looking building perched just on the edge of the wood planking.

Another chime above my head let me know I was still being surveyed.

It was weird that they were interested in something so mundane, but after my last call with my grandmother, maybe she'd called in some favors to up her surveillance.

I certainly wouldn't be calling anytime soon.

Will held the office door open for us, calling over my head into the dusty air, "Kelly, the spin-woman has arrived!"

A Latina woman with thick dark curls in a halo around her head looked up with a grimace as the door clanged shut behind us.

We both winced a second time as Evelyn, realizing that Will wouldn't be in the office with us, slammed back out the door.

"She thinks Will is hot," I said into the silence stretching between me and who I assumed was Kelly.

"I keep telling him to play up that angle for guests, but of course he only does it when I *don't* want him to." She stood and walked around the desk, shaking my hand with both of hers in earnest. "I'm Kelly Nerida."

"Caoimhe Ryan," I said. "And I'm so sorry, I'm actually a publicist."

She grinned and gestured to a chair across the desk from hers. "Apology accepted," she said, sitting back down in her own seat. "But I'm glad you're here regardless. I could use some advice. What's your hourly rate?"

I hesitated, standing still, twisting my fingers together.

I was never gonna get good at this part.

"Actually," I started but couldn't finish. I looked around Kelly's office, full of dust and rusting metal chairs. The walls were covered in sun-faded magazine photos and a few framed pictures of what appeared to be Kelly and Will, but that couldn't be right—they didn't look a day different in the photo but it was bleached as if it had been hung for decades. In one photo, they were shaking hands and Kelly was holding up a packet of papers in the air victoriously. In another, they were at the helm of a boat together, Will hamming as if he was Captain Morgan.

The filing cabinets behind Kelly that flanked the back wall all had crooked drawers and I wondered if they had ever worked properly. Her desk was barely treading water in a sea of paperwork, and a brick-thick laptop straight out of a '90s movie was propped open on one corner, humming loudly.

This was not a mega corporation with its own resources.

I looked back to Kelly, who had folded her hands on her desk and was watching me look around.

"The consult is free," I finally let out a breath and sat down. "Consider it a neighborly courtesy."

"We look that bad, huh?"

I started to stutter through a response but Kelly stopped me.

"It's that or Will charmed you *that* much as the new neighbor in the building and I know that's not it."

I laughed, feeling the nerves dissipate. I liked her, regardless of my misgivings about Will, and I leaned forward in my seat.

"So," I said. "Tell me about Mister Flipper."

When I finally left Kelly's office, I took a sharp right turn toward the end of the docks where the tour boats were floating, silent and huge above me. I fired off a quick text to my nine-thirty, apologizing for running late but asking to bump our call out. It was very nearly nine already and I was surprised to hear Eve's laughter coming high and clear from one of the boats.

"Evelyn Sharp, you're late for work!" I called without looking up from my phone.

"Caoimhe Ryan you're still here!" When I looked up, my best friend was peering down at me from over the railing of the boat in disbelief. Will poked his head up after her, throwing me a lazy wave.

And then a third face, one I didn't immediately recognize but guessed was the man of the hour—Leith.

I could see even from a distance that he was handsome, with a sharp nose and a gaze that made my heart stutter.

Shit.

If not working for companies was my guiding light, then not getting involved with clients was the star that kept me from Neverland. Besides, I had enough of human male disappointment that week.

"I'm looking for Leith," I called up. The third person nodded and disappeared from view.

"He'll be down," Will said. He went back to flirting with Eve who was laughing far too loudly for how funny he actually was.

"Evelyn go to work," I hollered, looking back down at my phone to answer my client's text.

I heard her sigh like an annoyed teen but the giggling faded and I expected to hear a quick goodbye from her as she headed to The Boston World offices.

"Who are you?"

I dropped my phone in surprise, looking up to see the stranger staring intently at me. He had slate grey eyes and he watched me from beneath bushy eyebrows. Like Will, he had dark shoulder-length hair that he let blow wild in the ocean breeze. But that was where the similarities ended. Where Will was ropey muscles and predatory grins, Leith was broad-shouldered and calm. He had an open face that he focused on holding in a serious pose, but I could see the beginnings of soft smile lines crinkling around his eyes. A dusting of stubble suggested distraction rather than carelessness and although he wore simple flannel and thick work pants, there were no holes or stains in his clothing.

Bending down to pick up my phone, I hastily pocketed it, sending up a silent thanks that it hadn't slipped through the planks and into the ocean—that was more than I needed for the morning.

"I'm Caoimhe," I said and offered my hand. He did not take it.

"Old country," he said. "Nice to meet you, Caoimhe."

He said my name right—like it was the most natural thing in the world. My breath caught in my chest.

"Could say the same for you, Leith." It felt like he was sizing me up. For what I didn't know. I had the wild, unsettling thought that maybe it was to eat me.

But no, where Will was simultaneously like a shark and a golden retriever—dangerous, playful, warm—his coworker was all wide-eyed tranquility. It was like being watched by a fish in an aquarium.

I finally let my hand drop awkwardly. "I'd like to talk to you about the incident yesterday," I said, slipping into my strongest business-woman armor. We didn't need to be friends, I just needed to know his side of the story so I could put together a plan.

Leith shrugged and looked down at his boots, a frown pulling at his face. "I was out of line," he said.

"It happens to the best of us," I offered.

"No," he shook his head. "No, it doesn't." He looked back up, fixing me with those startling eyes.

He waited, as if I was going to pass judgment on what was most likely a one-off behavioral issue. Kelly had briefed me on Leith's work history—quiet but efficient and at least courteous to guests. He never raised his voice or showed up late. Not so much as a complaint from a single person until yesterday.

"I promise it does," I said. "Did you feel you were provoked at all?"

Leith looked away, out toward the water. "He said something foul. I won't repeat it," he said.

"I'm not so delicate."

"He yelled at a kid."

"Sure, but—"

"He told her mermaids weren't real."

Above me, I heard my fairy tail gasp. Leith glanced up in its direction but then looked away again, so fast I wasn't sure it actually happened.

Desperate to cover up for the fairy above me, I leaned in toward Leith in what I hoped was a friendly, co-conspirator kind of way. "Well, I would've thrown him in the drink, too." I smiled my biggest, most winning smile.

Leith did not return it.

Damn, dude, give me something.

"No," he said, guilt flickering across his face. "You would've kept your cool."

"Don't underestimate me just yet," I said. Clearly, there was no way out of this but through. I pulled out my phone and opened up a new message. "I'm going to have you meet with a local emotions coach this week. What's your number so I can text you their information?"

"You want my number?" He sounded suspicious.

"I promise to only send nudes *after* your reputation is patched up." I rolled my eyes while inwardly cringing. Why was I letting this dude get to me? He beat up grumpy old men to preserve childhood innocence, sure, but that didn't make him a hero.

Incredibly, a hot red blush crept across his face, softening his features just enough that my heart clenched.

Well, that's not what I meant when I said give me something.

"I'm absolutely kidding, sorry that was—"

He took my phone, brushing a single calloused finger across my hand. I held in a shiver. I watched him tap each number, slowly and thoughtfully as if he had never given it out before. He handed my phone back and again, a light brush of his fingers sent jolts through my entire body.

"How fast can you patch up a reputation?" A flicker of a smile ghosted across his face and it was like a gut punch of serotonin.

"Well, that's really going to depend. You guys are in a pretty tough spot. Catching a bad rap right before tourist season closes? It'll be the first thing anyone remembers next summer and—" I was babbling and he had shut down, face held careful once more, the smile vanished.

"Anyway," I copied in Tony's coaching line and rates to a text, trying to keep my hands from shaking. I was being stupid. I wasn't even supposed to have taken this client and here I was bungling flirting with one of the crew.

Just breaking all the rules today. Let's rob a bank later and really go for it.

The text sent. I pocketed my phone.

"Call that number, tell him Caoimhe sent you," I said. "I have to get to another appointment but we'll be in touch. It was nice to meet you."

I set off at a quick pace down the docks, speeding away from our humiliating interaction.

Following the steps back down to the T station, only one thought bounced crystal clear through my mind, leaving me wondering exactly what I was hoping for:

I hope he calls.

6

Leith

The rest of the day passed in a blur. It was a sunny clear day and the last of the tourist crowd seemed dead set on getting their kicks before the fall winds blew in.

I was glad for the distraction.

"Don't underestimate me just yet."

I wouldn't—especially not with a royal Fae escort floating above her head. And there was no mistaking her birth status. Civilian unusualities like the rest of us didn't get Fae escorts.

Who was she?

There hadn't been anything strange about her, aside from the punch in my gut when we made eye contact. But that could've been anything—her bright hazel eyes, the long blonde curls breaking free from where she'd pinned them up, the way her jeans fit.

I shook my head, the way I'd been doing all day, trying to understand why she wouldn't get out of it.

I hadn't seen a fairy in a very long time—maybe mortal decades. They stayed hidden everywhere except the old country, and even there appearances were infrequent. Like the rest of us unusual creatures, they didn't want to be subjected to cruel human games for the sake of living true to themselves. Americans in particular didn't seem to have the respectful understanding needed when dealing with fairies—they had a creature that took teeth from children and left them *money* for fuckssake. Like a fairy would ever make a deal so nonchalantly.

Between dealings gone wrong with one too many inventors and the Industrial Revolution making iron more accessible, fairies had taken to the shadows, appearing only when called.

So why did a Boston PR woman have one following her around like she was the Queen herself?

Lost in thought, I found myself standing in front of Kelly's office, staring at the text from Caoimhe. The door swung open before I could knock.

"You can't date her."

I looked up at Kelly's stern face. She had her hands on her hips for emphasis but it was also blocking my way into the office.

"Who said anything about dating?" Will called from over her shoulder.

"I didn't." I held my hands out in peace.

"That's my man!"

"Will!" Kelly and I both said in the same exasperated tone.

"You better come in for this, Romeo." She turned and ushered me in, closing the door behind us.

The office was hot, with the windows closed and the sun beating in against the dust. I immediately wanted to leave, dread at the coming lecture and the stifling air making my heart beat loudly against my ribs.

Kelly pointed to Will. "I was just explaining why a mershark cannot get involved with a human woman. Did we all forget about Onda?"

"That's because men can't be trusted. The rule doesn't apply to women." Will was without his usual cigarette today, tapping his fingers against his seat with unchecked freneticism.

"First, Onda wasn't trapped by a man. And second, you think I couldn't do some damage?" Kelly arched an eyebrow.

"You're not human."

Kelly rolled her eyes and turned to me.

"Caoimhe is a stunner but you cannot get involved."

"I wasn't going to," I said. And it was true. But my own voice gave me away. If she'd kept flirting with me, I wouldn't have said no. Remembering her fairy companion I added, "Besides, I don't think Caoimhe is entirely human anyway."

Kelly and Will both stared for a moment.

"She had a fairy tail," I said, using the nickname for spying Fae. We'd twisted the name away from humans. If they were going to make up a bunch of nonsense about us for bedtime stories, we should at least get to reclaim it somehow.

Will threw his hands in the air like a football star making a touchdown. "I knew it! Old country name and a little something in the face. But that's even better! We don't have to tiptoe around her if she's one of us! And maybe Leith can get laid."

I frowned as Kelly laughed.

"Sorry, Leith." She squeezed my shoulder. "It would be nice for you to be a little less…" She gestured up and down at me and I wasn't sure if I should be offended or not.

"It's alright, buddy, I think the mopey look suits you." Will winked.

"I'm not dating anyone," I tried to protest.

Kelly nodded, putting a thoughtful hand to the side of her face. "And we don't know what the tail means."

Fear gripped my chest.

Don't say it.

"Come on, she's not…" Will's characteristic charm even faltered. He leaned forward in his seat. "A nice girl like that?"

Kelly nodded solemnly. "It's possible."

I had forgotten about the other reason for a tail—promised at birth.

It hadn't happened in a long time, but none of us had even *seen* a fairy in that long. Kelly wasn't wrong.

I felt a strange disappointment settle around my heart, as if the possibility of a day off had been replaced with a last-minute tour. It would be alright, so long as I didn't dwell too much on the original possibilities.

"I have to call a coach," I said, trying to change the subject.

"For your promising baseball career?" I shot Will a look and handed my phone to Kelly. I hated sports, which meant the entire city of Boston thought I was insane—Will included. He never missed an opportunity to tease me about it.

"It's an emotions coach," I said. "Caoimhe said it would help with whatever it is we're supposed to be doing."

"Good, I think you'll benefit from that for more than just PR reasons," she said, handing me back my phone. "And don't be tempted by having her number. I don't need you messing with claimed goods and coming back cursed after all this. We're lucky to have Caoimhe helping us."

"Man, I love having Leith yelled at for chasing tail instead of me."

Kelly threw her hands in the air.

"Alright, both of you out," she said and I could hear exhaustion in the edges of her words. "You are *both* well aware of the rules. Don't break them while we're cleaning up one mess already."

She rounded her desk as I opened the door and I caught her final desperate word as I stepped out into the late summer sun.

"*Please.*"

Once home, I found myself pacing, lapping each room in my apartment like I could measure the square footage with my body. I opened a beer which I abandoned on the counter in a puddle of condensation.

I wanted to be in the water. I *needed* to be in the water. But it wouldn't be safe until later—I had several hours to kill before the sun went down.

Now that I'd broken my literal dry spell, it was the only thing I could think about.

Well, not the *only* thing.

I stopped in the middle of my living room, looking around at the simple cheap furniture Will took me to buy with my first paycheck.

The truth was that we were on a path to repairing the damage I'd done yesterday. We were lucky it'd happened so fast—that Will lived next door to a publicist who hadn't already written him off as the drunk problem in the building. This was a *good* thing.

But dread coiled in my stomach like a snake waiting to strike.

I picked up my phone and looked at the text still open from Caoimhe.

If she really was promised to a Fae, did she know? What were the terms of the contract and who had made them for her? I wasn't an expert at Fae negotiation but I knew some who were. Maybe we could get her out of it and she could be free to—

I heaved a loud sigh and flopped on the couch.

I didn't own a TV, there was never anything on anyway, but for the first time I wished I did. I wanted a distraction from my whirling thoughts.

Besides, the chances were that she *was* Fae royalty and I didn't stand a chance with her anyway.

Not that I *wanted* the chance.

I stood up, grabbing my jacket and slamming the apartment door behind me. Maybe a walk would clear my head.

Before I knew it, I was walking along the river again, following the pull of the ocean in my gut. I found a bench and sat, watching the light through the trees that arched over the path, listening to the early fall breeze rattle through their branches.

The ocean knew I would come. But I would make it wait.

I thought about Onda.

She'd been an ambitious and outgoing mermaid, in love with human music and dancing. She'd met a human woman at a club and the two had gotten serious quickly. Caught in the whirlwind romance, Onda revealed her mermaid self to who she thought was the love of her life—and her love had promptly sold her to one of the massive research facilities in Boston.

We still didn't know where she was, even after several failed attempts to break in and find her. She must have been shipped someplace else. Someplace secret.

Someplace away from the ocean.

I shuddered.

I definitely would not risk getting involved with a human, Kelly was right.

My phone buzzed in my pocket.

Caoimhe: *What did Tony say?*

"Shit," I whispered to myself even as a warm joy spread to my limbs at seeing her name on my screen. "Shit shit *shit.*"

Me: *Nothing.*

Before I could shove my phone back in my pocket and try to forget about it, there was already a response.

Caoimhe: *We can't work to fix this if you don't get started. Tony is great. I never give clients bad recommendations. :)*

Caoimhe: *Would it help if I was on the first call to introduce you?*

"Fuck no." My outburst startled a passing jogger but I stopped myself from typing it out exactly.

Me: *No, it's okay.*

I tried not to get dizzy as Caoimhe's response came in before I was done. I needed this whole thing to slow down by about half.

Caoimhe: *Nope, wow, sorry that's a weird offer. I just meant I'm happy to make this feel easier in whatever way you need.*

Then my phone was ringing. It was Caoimhe. I lifted my arm up and stood, then physically forced myself to settle back down. I could not throw my phone in the river. I also couldn't ignore her call.

I picked up on nearly the last ring.

"Hey! I hope you don't mind, I thought this would be faster," she chirped into the phone, all cheery business. "It wasn't clear from your last text—is it okay to introduce you to Tony with me there or is it okay if I don't do that? I just want to make sure."

"It's okay," I said, suddenly struck dumb. I didn't care about the coach, I cared about knowing what her fucking deal was.

"Right," she paused. "Well, you just let me know. I'm here if you need me."

"Your friend," I stumbled, trying to catch her before she hung up.

"What about her?"

Shit, I didn't mean the girl Will was following around with his tongue out. I meant her tail but now I couldn't just blurt that out without complicating things.

"I think she's into Will, honestly," she said slowly, gently. I'd been silent too long and she thought I intended something else.

"It's okay," I said again.

"So you mentioned."

"I didn't mean her," I said, finally getting a grip on myself. "I meant someone else." Well, not a *good* grip.

"Uh huh," she sighed into the phone. "I don't date clients, it's a professional thing."

"That's not what I meant." Was it?

"Right, so you ask about my 'friend' but you don't mean my 'friend.'" I could hear the air quotes in her voice. This was not going well.

"I meant the coach." I didn't. I didn't mean any of these things. What was the fastest way to die on the spot?

"Tony," she said and now she sounded embarrassed. "Yes, sorry, obviously you meant Tony. What about him?"

"Do you know how late he works?" I wasn't going to call him today.

"Pretty late, especially for initial consults. Shoot him a text and ask," she said, her chipper voice pitched back into place. "I'll let you go so you can do that, have a great night!"

The line went silent. Apparently, she wanted out of that as desperately as I did.

I let out a deep breath, and texted Tony. Maybe if I did what she asked of me, I could limit our interactions and avoid any further embarrassment.

But as the text sent, I knew that wasn't what I wanted.

THE BOSTON WORLD

MISTER FLIPPER MAY PAY PRICE FOR FLIPPANT MISTER

Boston, MA. A normally sunny tour with long-time operator Mister Flipper took an unexpectedly violent turn yesterday in the Boston Harbor when a man was thrown overboard after a verbal altercation with a boat-hand escalated.

Bystanders said they saw the man say something to the boat-hand who immediately became agitated. Without warning, he grabbed the passenger and threw him bodily into the harbor. Multiple videos were captured of the conflict and have been circulating widely on social media platforms. Viewers have dubbed the boat-hand "Dunk Man" and have rapidly reinterpreted him into memes, trending audios, and one very intricate puppet re-enactment.

The victim was contacted for comment but prefers to remain anonymous at this time.

"I won't be pressing charges," they said to the World. "But I don't want anyone else to be attacked the way I was. I'd think twice before investing in Mister Flipper next summer."

Leadership at Mister Flipper was unavailable for comment by the printing of this article.

7

Caoimhe

"Of course he meant Tony." I let my phone drop onto the counter with a loud thud and put my head in my hands. Why had I assumed he was interested in a date and not the literal friend I told him to call for professional reasons?

Embarrassment had my entire body in a vice.

Not that this was entirely my fault. He could've been clearer. It was like more than two words at a time would make his head pop off.

I would've screamed in frustration but I didn't need Will poking his nose into anything else—or Pete knocking on my door twice in one week.

A chime-like giggle sounded from near my phone and I opened my eyes to the fairy who'd been following me all day.

"You," I growled. "I don't have time for this. What are you doing?"

They yelped as they dodged the flat of my hand.

"Please, Duchess! Dame Ryan worries about you!"

"She's got a funny way of showing it." I let my hair down and scrunched frustrated hands along my scalp. "I have to get ready for a client event. If I so much as *think* you're following me again, I will squash you."

The fairy stuck a miniscule tongue out at me, pulling a face. I clapped my hands near it and it vanished with a sudden popping sound.

One thing at a time. First, my writer client, Mirabel. She had her first reading in an hour and I needed to be there. I had a lucky streak I wasn't interested in ending.

Then, I needed to put together a strategy for Mister Flipper—at *least* a communication plan, but I had the feeling they'd need something bigger.

Somewhere in there would need to be dinner, a shower, and a glass of wine.

None of my priorities left room for further arguments with my grandmother.

Definitely no room for handsome tour boat operators.

"You don't even like the strong silent type," I hissed to myself as I threw open my closet and realized I hated everything I owned.

***

The bookstore was crowded, filled with students milling around on their way home from class. Slowly, as I helped Mirabel set her table with display books and posters, I noticed the average age of customer begin to increase. More and more people came in, hesitating in the doorway, unsure whether they should disappear among the maze of shelves or wait for further instruction.

I caught the eye of a clerk tidying up behind the register and she leapt into action, coming around the counter and ushering people toward the folding chairs spread around the front half of the store.

It wasn't a perfect set-up, but it was Harvard—Mirabel was beside herself with excitement.

She squeezed my hand as the room filled and the hour drew near. I squeezed it back, gave her my best "you'll be great" smile, and stepped away, giving the store manager room to begin.

I saw Evelyn sneaking past him, clearly having just entered. I didn't have time to process that Will and Leith were behind her as Mirabel's introduction started.

"Hi," Eve mouthed. I shot her a look, pointing with my chin at her guests but she only smiled wider. She was practically *glowing*. We'd have to talk about whatever the fuck this was later.

Mirabel stood, holding her book to her chest and looking around the room. She was wearing long, swirling purple layers that made her silver hair pop as the sun set behind her. Tinkling silver jewelry rang out from every free limb and I had to stop myself from scanning the air around us.

"Thank you all for coming," she said, beaming like an art teacher on the first day of school.

I watched for the tell-tale signs that my luck was in the room with us—more laughs than a passage deserved, longer applause than is expected, or a prestigious media critic smiling to themselves as they took notes.

There were no note-takers in the room as Mirabel began reading, her voice clear and strong like we'd practiced, but I noticed a palpable shift in the audience. People leaned forward in their seats, clutched one another's hands, smiled to one another at points where they related to the characters.

Mirabel, for her part, never stuttered or stumbled—what some would call a miracle given her nerves and lack of experience.

I knew better.

I took a deep breath and glanced over at my unexpected guests. Will and Evelyn were making eyes at one another, which seemed to be the only thing either of them was capable of over the last twelve hours. But Leith was listening to Mirabel like he just discovered books and nothing in his life could compare. He was stone-still, maybe not even blinking.

But it was the softness in his face that didn't just clench my heart, it threatened to suffocate it.

He *loved* this—whether it was Mirabel or the story or the bookstore. Whatever it was, he really, truly loved it and with such a yearning I was tempted to reach over and soothe him.

Or turn his head.

The thought came from seemingly nowhere. Cold fear sharpened in my gut and I thought my heart would slam through my chest. What would I even do if someone looked at me like that? Like they were truly seeing me—and they loved what they saw.

"You're something else, aren't you?"

Panic began to rise in my throat and I had to take deep breaths in and out of my nose. Leith looking up at my fairy tail earlier that day flashed through my mind.

Something was up with these new strangers in my life. And the potential was terrifying.

A sharp jab in my side made me flinch and I grabbed Eve's hand before she could poke me again. She wiggled her eyebrows at me suggestively and I squeezed her hand before dropping it. I had to behave with Mirabel watching. If she glanced over and thought I was bored, I'd really hurt her—and fail as her publicist at the same time.

I crossed my arms, focused on my breathing, and turned my attention back to Mirabel until the reading was over.

Applause swept the room in a fervor when she closed her book at last. People stood from their various perches around the bookstore and I could hear shouts of encouragement from the additional backroom behind us.

Will whistled from next to me and I could see Mirabel blushing even from across the room. Leith's face still held that same tenderness and for the briefest moment, he glanced toward me. I had the strangest sensation of looking out over the ocean on a calm, clear day when the sun lit the edges of the waves on fire with light.

But the moment was over before it started and Leith returned his attention to Mirabel. I couldn't breathe. My heart was going to explode. I had to get out of the room.

As calmly as I could, I nudged my way through the crowd. I blew a kiss to Mirabel and pointed toward the door, letting her know I wasn't going far.

Outside, I gulped in the cool air, shrugging out of my jacket to let it wash over my bare shoulders. I'd opted for a tank beneath my favorite cool-chic cropped leather jacket and I'd been comfortable until just that moment.

What was happening to me?

Maybe it was time for a vacation.

Before I could straighten my thoughts out like I wanted, Eve blew through the door with Will close behind her, the noise from inside washing out onto the sidewalk around us as a few other guests made their way home.

"What a find, C!" Eve threw her arms around me in a celebratory hug before pulling away, concern pulling her face down. "You okay?"

I nodded, forcing a smile. "It's just too warm in there, that's all."

Doubt flickered across her face, but Eve let it go, dropping the hug but taking my hand instead. It was fortifying, her soft hand in mine, the familiar press of the many rings she wore between my fingers.

"Are you mad I brought Will and Leith?" she nodded her head toward Will, who lit a cigarette. "I figured they could use a little culture, help soften 'em up for your image rehabilitation."

"Leith is already a big artsy fartsy squish," Will said, exhaling smoke. "He lives for this shit."

"Really?" Eve and I were surprised in unison.

"He might look tough, but he's nothing but poetry and soft music on his insides. Not that I need to tell you that." He winked at me.

"What—"

"We saw the way you were looking at him in there."

"I'm impressed you saw anything. I assumed you were too busy trying to fuck Eve's face with your eyes."

"I'd like to fuck her face with more than my eyes."

Eve let out a joyous shriek and smacked him on the shoulder. Will's smile was sharp but playful, and for the first time, I thought less of a shark looking at him.

I stuck my tongue out at both of them in annoyed disgust.

Mirabel's silvery head appeared from around the corner of the door. "Caoimhe!" She smiled and gestured me to come in. "Wonderful news!" Then, dropping her voice to a stage whisper, she continued, "There's an agent. From *Hollywood.*"

There it was. My luck had done its job.

I let go of Eve's hand, shrugging back into my jacket as I slipped back into my publicist self. Entering the bookstore, I caught Will and Eve standing close, nose to nose, giggling over something.

We were *definitely* going to have a lot to talk about later.

8

Leith

It was sheer luck that Will called right after Caoimhe, demanding I do something other than "sit around and sulk all night." Admittedly, my couch had looked like the best prospect for the evening, so I agreed to go with him and Eve to a debut author reading.

I should've suspected they were up to something when we walked in and Caoimhe was standing in the back of the room, her curls glowing around her face in the slanted evening light. It was all I could do not to stare at her the entire time, so I let myself drop into the author's work instead.

The woman's book spoke of joy in the face of loss, of the triumph in a sunny morning after a storm. I felt it seep into my bones and settle there, drifting along the bottom of my own personal ocean. It was refuge and comfort without hiding from pain.

Once again, human art reminded me why it was worth fighting against the pull of the ocean to return forever, why I would continue to hide among them if it meant nights like this.

At one point, I was sure I could feel Caoimhe's eyes on me, threatening to burn right through to my core but still I stayed my course. It was only the final moment I caved to temptation and whatever she saw in me drove her from the room with force.

She had to know what I was. She knew and was horrified. There was no other explanation for it.

When I saw her come back into the bookstore, her usual confidence and calm restored, I stepped behind a shelf to avoid staring. The pull this woman had on me was stronger than any current and I would need physical anchors to keep from being dragged down.

I was too busy trying to catch my breath to notice what aisle I'd ducked into until Will appeared by my side and let out a low whistle.

"Anarchy and Philosophy," he said and I turned to see his trademark sharp smile aimed right at me. "Whale shark's got some teeth after all. I was gonna suggest we all go for a beer, but maybe you'd rather throw bricks through storefronts?"

I resisted the urge to punch him.

"A beer would be great." Maybe some time with Will would help me refocus. I could convince him to finally go for a swim, or ask him what he thought he was doing directly ignoring Kelly's orders not to fool around with human women. I followed Will out of the bookstore and onto the sidewalk, grateful for some time with him. But then I noticed Caoimhe was right behind us. My nerves pulled under my skin in panic.

"Ready, ladies?" Will looped an arm around Eve with an easy confidence. It made me ache and I found my gaze drifting again to Caoimhe who was looking down the street.

Maybe a beer wouldn't be so great.

Eve and Will led us to an unassuming pub a few blocks over, leaving Caoimhe and I to follow awkwardly in silence. The pub was all brick and dark wood finishes with a chalk sign over the bar listing specials in someone's crooked handwriting. Several grey-haired men in flannels sat in the far corner, so we opted for a table closer to the front.

Again, Will and Eve left us, ordering at the bar and waited for the drinks while Caoimhe stared at her phone and I stared at her. I racked my brain to think of something to say but all I could come up with was

"I texted Tony," I said, feeling it flop in the air before it had a chance.

Caoimhe didn't look up but nodded. "He's great," she said, eyes still on her phone. She was using her client voice, smooth and high-pitched. *Cold.*

It felt like a year before Will and Eve returned with brown glass bottles for everyone. Eve held hers up and Caoimhe finally set her phone down.

"To Mirabel!" Eve cheered, and we all clinked our bottles together. A soft smile settled across Caoimhe's face and I pushed down the swirling in my stomach at the sight of it.

"So," Will set his beer down after taking a big swig. "Tell us what you're thinking for Mister Flipper."

Caoimhe looked thoughtful over her beer before answering.

"We'll definitely need a communication plan," she said. "An interview at The World to address the video now that it's officially viral."

"What does that mean?" I asked.

"Leith's afraid of the internet," Will mock-whispered across the table, earning a giggle from Caoimhe. I tried not to be jealous.

"It means that more than two million people have seen you throw that man into the harbor since yesterday," she answered, shooting me a look across the table. "It will be more by the time we all wake up tomorrow."

"I'm texting Gary at the News desk now," Eve said as her fingers flew across her phone screen.

"While Leith gets some coaching, we should think about ways we can demonstrate to the community that everyone has learned their lesson and Mister Flipper is dedicated to continued betterment."

My head was swimming. It suddenly felt like a lot of work to clean up over my singular stupid action.

"Tony's company has a good reputation with some major players here in town," Caoimhe continued, barely taking a breath. "I'd like to see, after he meets with Leith, if he'd be willing to co-sponsor an event together. With a development company's name on the banner, people will see you're serious about managing yourselves going forward."

She was talking like I wasn't there, looking only to Will. He *was* the co-founder but I still felt small, like I should be under the table while the adults were talking.

I took another sip of my beer and tried to remember how I'd gotten myself into this situation.

"What about a carnival?" Eve sat up straight in her chair. "The tour guides can run games and give out kettle corn and we can set up a dunk tank—"

"No dunk tank," Will and I both said automatically.

Caoimhe looked at me like she was trying to read a headline in a foreign language, as if my face would offer context clues for what was really happening.

Eve shrugged. "Okay, no dunk tank—but definitely still games and popcorn."

Caoimhe was nodding at Eve, her gaze cloudy and unfocused. "It shows a playful and approachable side of the company that people might not get just from taking a tour," she said slowly. "It could help with next year's season, too."

"We'll have to see what Kelly thinks," Will said.

"I'll come by tomorrow afternoon and we can pitch her." Caoimhe set down her half-empty beer and stood. "I'm going home to write this all down before I forget."

"Leith, walk her home," Will said, looking at Eve like he might devour her the second I was gone.

"No," Caoimhe and I both said together.

"I'll be fine," she said.

"I don't mind," I offered.

We locked eyes for just a moment before she glanced away again.

"It's not far," she said and I wasn't sure if it was a concession or not.

"It'll make me feel better," Eve said, touching Caoimhe's wrist lightly. Caoimhe nodded then looked up at me finally.

"Alright," she said. "Thank you."

Outside the sky was a bright purple, clinging to the last of the sun as it finished setting. Caoimhe and I walked again in silence for several blocks before she heaved a loud sigh.

"What kind of poetry do you like?" She asked like it pained her to know.

"How do you know I read poetry?"

"You don't have to tell me."

"All of it, I guess." I thought for a moment. "John Glenday, Rudy Francisco, good ol' Rabbie Burns."

"Who?"

"He's a favorite fellow Scotsman."

"You're Scottish?"

"Leith didn't give it away?" I was smiling wide, relief flooding my system. We were finally talking in a way that bordered on comfortable.

"So then you know I'm Irish, because surely Caoimhe gave it away," she said, mocking me lightly. It tickled something hot and low in my gut.

We turned down a street lined with the short two-story brick buildings that always turned my mind to stories of war and rebellion. The ironwork lanterns hanging low above us were filled with electric bulbs instead of candles, but the impact was immediate.

"We're kindred in solidarity at least, then. Unless you hate me." I hoped it sounded like a joke, but even *I* could hear the desperation in my voice.

Caoimhe stopped and turned to me, eyes wide with concern. "Do you think I hate you?"

I didn't know what to say. *Yes. Obviously. Who wouldn't?*

"Leith, I don't hate you," she said, her voice hushed, and hearing her say my name like that sent a jolt into every part of my body. Despite myself, I felt my cock twitch. I wanted to lean in to hear her better, to get closer to the rush of air coming from her lips but I was frozen in place.

How do you feel then?

"I don't scare you?" I asked, my voice tight in a way I was sure would give me away.

"Oh you do," she said and grinned at me, a light dancing in her eyes. "I don't want to get thrown in the harbor next."

I wanted to kiss her then, caught in the streetlights, surrounded by history as the sun set behind us and she was finally smiling up at me.

And *holy shit* she was looking at my mouth too.

"I'm only two doors up from here," she said. "So this should probably be goodbye."

"Just goodnight," I said. *Never goodbye, please gods, never goodbye.*

She nodded, stepping away and putting space between us. It felt it like a punch to the chest.

"Just goodnight, then, Leith." She waved to me and I watched her walk away, as if I could memorize her every detail before she disappeared behind a door.

"Goodnight," I called back before heading directly for the harbor.

I needed to cool off, immediately.

9

Caoimhe

I woke up the next morning determined to focus solely on work and *not* on Leith.

His full attention on me beneath the streetlight last night had *not* fried my entire brain and the mere sight of his lips had *not* turned me on in an almost painful way.

This was *fine.* I was in complete control and nothing was going to derail me.

My phone rang as soon as I sat down with my laptop.

"Hello grandmother," I said, tapping the speaker icon so I could begin formatting the Mister Flipper communication plan. If she was going to yell at me, I was going to get work done while she did it.

"Caoimhe Ryan, why am I hearing you've been fraternizing with merfolk?"

I was sure Will heard me laughing across the landing.

"Because the tail you hired is confused," I said.

"Stop clacking away on that machine and listen to me."

"Girl's gotta pay her bills, Nan."

"We've discussed your impertinence, young lady," she hissed through the phone.

"Sorry—a girl's gotta pay her bills, Dame Ryan."

"You wouldn't have to pay bills at all if you would return where you're needed."

"Tempting but no thank you." I began typing out a short summary at the top of the plan that would help steer the rest of the document. I was lost in it for a few minutes before I realized my grandmother was still on the phone.

"—dragging you down to the depths because you can't contain yourself."

"I'm a strong swimmer, grandmother, please don't worry." I picked up the phone and continued before she could cut me off. "But I really do have work to finish today, we'll talk later. Bye, Nan." I tapped to end the call and set the phone back down, returning to the communication plan.

"Merfolk," I huffed to myself. "Seriously?"

A few hours later, a full plan written out and an interview arranged with Eve's colleague, the full impact of what my grandmother had said hit me.

I spit out my oatmeal, nearly choking.

Why did I think it was insane that merfolk existed? *Of course* they existed. Had she meant Leith? I thought back to the sensation of staring across the ocean when we made eye contact. But no. Merfolk were dangerous flesh-eating monsters, not poetry-reading tour boat guides.

I'd never met one in real life, but I heard stories—friends lost to a friendly smile too far beyond the waves, children disappearing from the side of boats because they leaned down too close to the "pretty lady." Merfolk weren't the singing beauties human movies made them out to be. They were vicious flesh-eaters with no care or concern for humans as more than meal. So rarely did the magical world I moved through present itself as a true danger, but when it did…

Will's shark-like smile and watery eyes hit me like a bullet train.

"Oh no," I hissed, standing in a rush to throw open my front door. "Evelyn."

I was across the landing in a flash, pounding on Will's door like a woman possessed until I realized that he was most likely at work.

Full from a good dinner, I thought to myself. Sprinting back into my apartment, I almost couldn't get my phone unlocked with my shaking fingers. I tapped Eve's name and held my breath while it rang.

"Wildly successful and well-dressed Evelyn Sharp at your service," she answered and I nearly passed out from relief.

"You're okay," I gasped.

"Better than okay." I could hear her grinning through the phone. "I have so much to tell you. You're going to *die* when you hear what Will and I did last night."

"Evelyn, *no.* He's dangerous."

Silence.

"C, where is this coming from?" Her voice lost its charm, growing defensive.

"I can't really explain, I just need you to trust me."

"Caoimhe Ryan." Her tone was stern, like she was lecturing a small child. "Do not go projecting *your* trust issues onto the first man who has made me happy in a long time."

"Eve—"

"*No,*" she hissed. "Figure your own shit out before you come for mine. You don't even really date! When was the last time you let someone get to know you passed two dates and a quick fuck?"

"Aren't you at work?" I could barely breathe.

"It's a newsroom, C, like anyone gives a shit about my language. Answer the question."

"Eve that's not what this is about, seriously. I know something about Will that—"

"Answer. The. Question."

I sighed. Evelyn could be like a lion with a carcass when she wanted something—teeth sunk in bone deep, refusing to let go.

"You know me," I answered.

"I'm not fucking you, try again."

I didn't have an answer.

"Will you at least hear me out?" I pleaded. I had no idea how I was going to explain this to her. But something in my gut told me that maybe it was time to come clean to Evelyn—about everything. She was right. I'd been hiding, even from her. And why?

"I can't bear to lose another member of our family the way we lost your father." My grandmother's words rang through my head. A swell of grief threatened to overwhelm me, replaced quickly with full-body fear at the possible pain I could face. I shook my head to clear the thoughts away.

There were a lot of people in this world who would try to hurt me if they knew the truth—what I could do, who I was. Evelyn Sharp was not on that list.

"Tell you what," the mischief was back in Eve's voice and I braced myself. "You go out with Leith for one drink—just the two of you and you have to *actually* talk to him—and I will listen to whatever it is you need to tell me about Will."

"And you'll consider it seriously." I added. I could almost hear Eve nodding.

"Duh, C."

I sighed. "Fine. It's a deal."

Eve squealed with joy and I heard a man's voice in the background telling her to knock it off. She pulled the phone away and I heard her faintly responding in a foul way that would've gotten anyone else fired. How she kept her job continued to mystify me.

"I'll see you at Mister Flipper after work," she said. "I'm meeting Will and he'll bring Leith. Then it's up to you two to figure out your date."

"Wait, Leith is in on this?" My body went hot and cold at the same time. I couldn't tell if I was terrified or giddy with joy.

"Nope!" she chirped. "He's going to be just as annoyed as you are, but you two need to get over yourselves. I'm sure you can help each other in *certain ways*. See you!"

The line was silent before I could protest. After all, I'd already promised. And if anyone was going to hold me to my word, it would be my best friend in the entire world.

I looked down at the phone in my hand and tried not to feel as if I'd just been plunged into the deep end of chaos.

***

Kelly loved the carnival idea. She was ecstatic, pacing from one end of the office to the other as she spouted off plans for the games, the prizes they could offer, and even went so far as to call someone she knew who owned a carousel.

She kicked me out of the office for that part.

"It's a subculture Slavic dialect, and I get nervous speaking it in front of people if you wouldn't mind," she gestured toward the door. "Thank you Caoimhe. Seriously. You're saving us."

I waved and closed the door behind me on what sounded like an ear-piercing series of shrieks—or maybe that was just what my untrained ear heard.

Just in time, I heard the clattering footsteps and chatter of guests getting off the last tour of the day. Will's raucous laughter sounded from someplace out of sight and as I walked closer, squinting against the late sun, there was Leith by the gangplank, seeing everyone off. As I watched, an elderly woman, crooked and shaking, placed a hand on Leith's arm as she approached the exit. He leaned into her, listening, and then *actually smiled*.

I couldn't look away. I'd never seen him smile before and it spread across his face, crinkling his eyes, dimpling his cheeks. Even his shoulders relaxed, dropping down to a comfortable height. It was like looking at an entirely different person.

An even more handsome person.

"Stop that," I breathed to myself.

"Stop what?"

I shrieked, clamping a hand over my mouth and snapping my gaze away to Evelyn standing next to me.

"You need a bell!"

"When I've got these creaky ol' planks to announce my presence like a true queen?" She swept a dramatic hand toward her feet.

"You scared me." My heart was racing, and I couldn't quite see straight. Which was definitely from being startled and nothing else.

"Not my fault you were so deep in a Mr. Darcy moment you didn't hear me coming."

I shot her a look and shook my head.

"You know," she continued, ignoring me. "Mr. Darcy is so consumed with love for Lizzie Bennet he can't even speak so he just stares awkwardly and she assumes it's because he thinks she's disgusting."

"He calls her tolerable."

"Yeah, and then he bails out her stupid sister and writes her the *best* love letter. Not something you do for someone you think is tolerable. He's just socially inept."

Eve and I were perpetually having this argument and now was not when I wanted to continue it.

"I don't know which part of this I'm supposed to be flattered by."

"None of it!" She threw an arm over my shoulder and nudged me toward the tour boat, swinging her legs lazily as we walked. "Are you ready for your date?"

Will howled from the deck, leaning over the railing toward us and saving me from having to answer.

"Who let the models off the runway?"

Eve giggled and let me go, giving her best catwalk along the pier and right up the gangplank.

Will scooped her up and spun her around. I had to look away when they started kissing, blushing hard. I wasn't sure if it was confusion at seeing Eve so enthusiastic or the sudden daydream slip I had at the romantic gesture.

Get it together.

Leith was still standing by the gangplank and he looked as confused as I was. He cleared his throat aggressively and arched his eyebrows. When Will surfaced for air he gave him a one-armed wave, still clinging to Eve with the other.

"Go on, ya ol' grump. Evelyn and I will finish." The suggestion was enough to inspire another wave of giggles from Eve and I tried not to roll my eyes. I was glad she was excited about a new guy but this was ridiculous.

"Gross," I called up and Eve threw me a wink over Will's shoulder, sticking her tongue out.

"Go get your own!" She called.

"But not before we get ours!" Will bodily lifted Eve up and over his shoulder then, giving her ass a slap and strutting off. Eve shrieked and waved goodbye, her whole face alight as they disappeared toward the back of the boat.

Leith looked lost, stuck near the gangplank, a small metal counter still gripped in his hand. I took a few steps forward, stopping at the base of the ramp and looked up at him.

"If we go get a beer, we can plead innocence when they're caught doing illegal things on a boat."

He looked at me like he was seeing me for the first time—like I hadn't been real until right then. It made my skin tingle in a not-unpleasant way.

Don't let him look too closely.

I took a breath and let it out slowly. If he didn't say anything in the next five seconds—

"A beer would be great." And there again was the smile, wholeheartedly crinkling and dimpling.

"Okie dokie!" *Kill me.*

FROM MISTER FLIPPER FOR IMMEDIATE RELEASE

Boston, MA. On Friday's mid-day tour, one of our employees entered into an altercation with a guest resulting in that individual's forcible ejection from the boat into the harbor. These actions are inexcusable and dangerous, and Mister Flipper extends our sincerest apologies to the guest, their family, and all other guests aboard the tour that day who bore witness to the altercation.

Mister Flipper is a family-run business and has been in operation in Boston for more than 40 years. We have grown and thrived in the harbor thanks to the continued patronage of our guests, but also the hard work of our crew. We would not be where we are today without our tour boat operators, and we believe in taking care of one another.

As such, we have asked the offending employee to participate in regular counseling sessions and have relieved him of any duties that may aggravate poor emotional regulation while he continues to learn stronger coping strategies. Additionally, we are exploring partnerships with Boston-local mental health experts to ensure all members of our company are better equipped for high-stress situations aboard any vessel.

We understand this is unconventional, but Mister Flipper is not an average business with average employees. We are so much more than that, and we hope our actions reflect that back to our valued community and guests.

10

Leith

I followed Caoimhe like a lost dog, down the harbor, across a bridge, and up the elevator to a swanky business building overlooking the water. I kept an eye out for her Fae escort but it never appeared. Either they had the day off, or I'd miscalculated Caoimhe's standing. Would an important member of a Fae court be left unattended with a stranger if she was promised to another?

Probably not.

I couldn't contain the leap my heart did at the thought.

We stepped out onto the top floor of the building, entering a trendy bar filled with well-dressed people lounging on steel-grey all-weather sofas beneath patio heaters. The sun was sinking low in the sky as Caoimhe picked a small table in a corner of the deck, a little quieter as the breeze picked up the music and whisked it away.

"I hope you don't mind, I love the view even if it's a little chilly this time of year."

I nodded dumbly. She clasped her hands together, her client smile stuck on her face. "Great, I'll grab us some drinks then."

"No." If this was supposed to be a date, then I should be buying. Right?

"Oh," she paused, brow furrowing. "I'm so sorry, I just assumed. I'm sure they have some delicious non-alcoholic options, I'll ask."

I was torn between saving the spot she'd picked out and following her to pay for the drinks at the bar. The patio was crowded and by the time the thought crossed my mind, all the other tables filled.

"Shit," I whispered. Now there wouldn't even be alcohol to steel my nerves. I took a deep breath and sat down.

While I waited, a crew of boisterous men in suits stream onto the patio. They were talking and joking loudly with one another, shrugging off jackets and loosening ties as they milled around. None of them seemed particularly interested in choosing a seat, standing directly in all the spaces designed for walking through.

I saw Caoimhe's curls appear over shoulders briefly as she navigated the sudden crowd, then the rest of her emerged, holding a simple brown liquor in a glass and something dramatically decorated with an umbrella and stacks of fruit. I held back a grimace at my impending smoothie.

Just as Caoimhe seemed to be free of the suited gathering, a careless arm smacked into her, sloshing both drinks all over the floor.

I half-stood, unsure if I should intervene as Caoimhe closed her eyes for a moment. The offending arm-swinger turned around and had the sense to apologize. I couldn't hear them over the music, but she appeared to shrug him off then gestured toward me. I raised my hand to wave in acknowledgment then lowered it as I saw recognition dawn on his face.

How could this guy know me?

And then I remembered the whole reason Caoimhe and I met in the first place.

I watched, rooted to the spot, as the man tapped several shoulders in the crowd, pointing directly at me. Before anyone else could be alerted, Caoimhe sprang into action. She handed the half-empty drinks to one of the other men in the crowd, who accepted them while distracted staring at me. She didn't run but walked calmly and quickly to our table where she looped an arm through mine and guided me back toward the exit.

"Brace yourself," she said, low and close in my ear. I held in a shiver at the heat of her breath on my skin. This was not the time or place. "There's only one way out of here, but I've got you. Just focus on my voice."

I was all too happy to listen to Caoimhe talk low only to me for the rest of the night but the force of the crowd slammed into me hard and loud.

"Eyyy, Dunk Man!"

"You spilled his girl's drink, bro, he's gonna dunk you next!"

"Sick, dude, he's so chill in real life."

"Hey Dunk Man!"

"Can we get a selfie?"

"Yo that's Dunk Man!"

When we finally broke through the other side, I was dazed, certain I'd entered another reality. I let Caoimhe lead me to the elevator. It wasn't until the doors shut and we were left in silence that I finally exhaled.

Caoimhe started to let go of my arm but I put my free hand on hers and squeezed. Her hands were soft beneath mine.

"Please," I breathed. "Just a moment longer."

She was warm against me as she leaned her head on my shoulder. She smelled clean and bright, like laundry in the sun but with something floral and soft. I stopped myself from inhaling her too deeply, painfully aware of how silent it was in the elevator, of how hard my breathing had become in just a few steps through the crowd.

When the doors pinged open, I let go of her hand but her arm stayed looped through mine. Warm joy spread through me as I realized she wasn't letting go.

"I'm sorry," she said as we stepped back out onto the street. "What a mess."

"You didn't know," I offered.

"Yes, but I should've. I shouldn't have picked such a popular place since your video is still trending." She heaved a sigh. I prayed she didn't feel my arm twitch as I resisted the urge to wrap her close to me, to soothe the worry from her face.

"It's okay," I said. Did she hear the tension in my voice? Did she know how much work it was to "play it cool" like Will had told me to not even an hour prior?

"We can call it a night if you want, I don't want to torture you any further."

She had no idea. And yet.

"I'm up for a little more torture," I said, steering our steps away from the water and further into the city. "I know a place."

We walked the short few minutes in silence, and I took the opportunity to slip my hand into hers, running my thumb along the soft skin there. My mind wandered at the touch, imagining other soft places I could trace with my fingers, all too aware of how my rough my callouses were in comparison. I glanced at her face to find a glow in her cheeks.

Did she like it?

We reached the front door of the quiet little brewery I favored when Will was on a dry kick. He was always dragging me into smokey dives with other weathered dockworkers. He said the brewery was for hipsters who weren't cool enough to work as artists, but I liked the soft light and hoppy beer.

Caoimhe stopped me before we could go in, pulling me toward her slightly.

"Wait," she said and let my hand go. I immediately wanted to grab it back but resisted. "I need to announce something so I can get it out of my system."

I froze.

She took a deep breath and in a single exhale said, "You make me incredibly nervous and it's distracting to both my professional and personal life but I would very much like to continue this date anyway but if I'm acting weird, please don't hold it against me I promise I will chill the fuck out shortly."

I laughed. I couldn't help myself. All my concerns evaporated.

"Me too," I said. "But I hope it's in a good way."

She nodded, her shoulders sagging in relief. "It is. Now let's get a goddamn drink."

I grinned, following her inside.

11

Caoimhe

The only piece of good advice my grandmother ever gave me was naming of a thing allowed you to cease being controlled by it—whether that was fear, anxiety, or a particularly cunning gremlin who wanted your first-born. While I was sure she meant it more for dealing with my fellow Fae, I often applied the logic to intense emotions with success.

And thank god because I couldn't take anymore spilled drinks or tense conversations.

As soon as I admitted being nervous, I saw Leith relax a little, felt my own shoulders release. He'd been good natured all evening, and I was surprised—though I don't know what else I expected. Despite his recent incident, he didn't strike me as ill-tempered.

"Just a moment longer."

He'd really been shaken up by the crowd on the rooftop. I tucked away the guilt pinging through my gut after the first beer, deciding to berate myself later when I wasn't having such a wonderful time.

I was also surprised by how much I was enjoying him touching me.

I wasn't usually a public displays of affection type of person. But with Leith, it was such a small thing—a brush of my knuckles with his fingertips, a shoulder bumping mine. I found myself sitting on the same side of the table as him, a gag-worthy maneuver that I didn't even realize happened until our knees were bumping.

He reached across the table to resume holding my hand, rubbing his thumb across it like he had when we walked. I could've just let him do that all night.

Such a small thing, but it inspired such a deep hunger. All those small touches kept building under my skin until every part of me was on fire, desperate to be smothered by his hands.

After the second beer, he dropped his hand to my knee and rested it there, warm through my jeans. My nerves fluttered from my stomach up my throat then back again. I had to resist the urge to wiggle under his touch to try and get more of it—to get it *higher.* I felt like I was going to combust.

But still, a small voice kept whispering in the back of my mind, *don't let them look too close.*

I thought about Eve on the phone that morning, chiding me for projecting my trust issues. As if she really knew why I stayed so hidden from the men I dated—as if she could have *any* idea.

We were on our third beer and I was starting to get desperate, his hand tracing lightly on my inner thigh while he told me about an exhibit on Impressionism he'd seen recently. How could he talk about painting techniques when his firm, thick fingers were a breath away from my pussy? Everything from my waist down was molten lava. If I moved I would erupt. If Leith didn't at least make out with me I was going to have to excuse myself to masturbate before I died from pent-up lust.

RIP Caoimhe Ryan. She tried to change her dating habits and it literally killed her.

My thoughts were running rampant, finding loopholes in the protective armor I'd built around my life. So what if I fucked another human? He couldn't be any more disappointing than the last few.

I glanced down at Leith's crotch, no longer caring if I was being obvious. A thrill ran down my spine and despite all my efforts, I shivered.

No. He would *not* be a disappointment.

"So you and Will," I started, trying to cover my obvious bodily reaction to him. I saw a flicker of concern across his warm expression. "How do you two know each other?"

"School friends," he said.

"Where'd you go?"

He paused, looking away from me. "Do you think we could be something?"

"Excuse me?" I was not going to assume that question was directed at me—we played that mortifying game on the phone already.

He looked back up and his gaze was heavy, stormy eyes dark. "You and me," he said.

"Are you trying to lock this in before you even kiss me?" I asked, incredulous. Talk about old school. And here I was trying to figure out the quickest way to a bedroom. "Or are you just avoiding the question?"

He braced an arm across the back of the booth, leaning in until we were barely a whisper apart.

"Why not both?" he murmured, dangerously close to my lips. I could smell him, musky and warm, baked in salt and sun.

"I'll get an answer eventually." What was I asking? I couldn't remember. Everything was Leith's scent and heat and mouth.

"Eventually," he repeated, but stayed where he was, teasing me the way he'd been teasing me all night. His hand stayed loose on my thigh, but it had edged up further than before. Was he torturing me or waiting for my move?

Fuck it.

I rushed in, closing the final gap between us, pressing my mouth to his. He sighed into the kiss, and I took the opening, slipping in my tongue as I slid my hands up into his hair, tugging at the roots. He deepened the kiss, sucking on my tongue before pulling back to nip at my bottom lip, which made me moan quietly into his mouth.

I was going to crawl on top of him in this bar. That would be the end of my career—no one would hire a publicist arrested for public sex.

Before I could make headlines, he pulled away, cupping my face with his hand and running that perfect, infuriating calloused thumb across my jaw.

"Should we go?" His voice was rough as his eyes searched my face.

"Duh," I said, immediately standing up and throwing my coat on.

"We should—"

I grabbed him by the collar and kissed him again, savoring the way he melted into it, first surprised then delighted.

"Fuck the tab," I said and hauled him with me out onto the sidewalk. He could come back for his card. I was sure he was the type to tip 20% or higher anyway.

It was cold enough outside that I was sure steam was wafting off my vibrating skin, need creating a haze between our bodies.

"Yours or mine?" I wanted to drag him into the alley directly to our right, but I thankfully had enough sense to remember the scene at the rooftop bar. Getting caught having sex in public was career-ruining but add in an internet celebrity who was also a client and it was *life*-ruining.

He considered me for a moment and I did my best not to squirm under his gaze.

"Yours," he said. "If that's alright?" There was a restraint in the question—not waiting for rejection so much as checking in.

"It's perfect," I said, tapping on my phone to call a ride. Was I about to be "that girl" in the ride-share making out in the backseat? Pussy clenching members of the audience say yes.

"Five minutes?! What are you doing, running errands on the way?"

There again was a calloused hand on my skin, rubbing lightly along the base of my skull and down my neck.

"Caoimhe," his voice dropped to a murmur and I swore to god I could feel it in my spine.

I looked up to see his jaw clenched, eyes worried.

"Oh," I said and let my shoulders drop. "Okay. I get it. Don't worry about it." Of course, he changed his mind. I rushed things and made him nervous.

Or he thought I was a whore.

I tried to step away but his hand kept me in place, gentle but firm.

"You didn't even hear what I was going to say."

"You don't have to come over."

"Yes, I do," he said and let out a soft laugh that hit me low and hot. *God damn it.* "If I don't, I'll be kicking myself for the rest of my life."

"But?" There always was one in conversations like this.

"I'm not going to have sex with you tonight."

It took every ounce of my adult self-control not to stamp my foot on the ground and whine.

"Please sir," I turned into him, mockingly offended while sliding my hands up his chest— Jesus Christ boat operators were ripped. "Don't take me for such a wanton tartlet. I simply wanted to offer the gentleman a bowl of porridge on this chilly evening."

He was looking down at me with such a heat and unwavering focus I almost stepped back. *Oh, so that's how it is. A little turn-of-the-century role play.*

"I've heard stories about your oatmeal," he said, voice tight but playful, rumbling through his chest where I was pressed. "And that's not the dish I hope to lap up tonight."

"Well now I'm confused. You said—"

"Let me be clear, Caoimhe," he still hadn't broken eye contact. His fingers slid up from the back of my neck into my hairline sending delicious waves of tingling nerves across my scalp and this time I couldn't stop the full body shiver. I was going to purr out loud. "I'm not going to have sex with you tonight because I don't want to rush. When you're presented with a masterpiece, you don't spend five minutes and move on."

"Five minutes?" I asked, breathless despite myself. If he was trying to tell me he had problems lasting, this was a helluva way to do it.

"You take your time. You give attention to every detail. You savor every second."

The car pulled up but I couldn't move, frozen to the spot by his gaze.

"I need to savor you, Caoimhe, before I can fuck you like I want to."

"Get in the car," I managed to say without stuttering.

I was definitely going to make out with him in the car.

***

The first time you bring someone home, there's always a moment when the door opens and the lights click on, that you see your own apartment as if for the first time—as if through their eyes. You notice for the first time how strange the furniture is laid out, or you get a swell of pride at the tasteful art on the walls. The layout you take for granted suddenly offers mysterious corners and surprises behind every door. It's usually only a moment and then it passes.

But when I brought Leith home, I was suddenly painfully aware of every messy pile, every crack, every chip. My couch looked dingy, the sliding door was covered in my fingerprints and an entire bag of flour had been ripped open across my kitchen floor.

"Wait, what the hell?"

As soon as I turned the corner to get a better look past the half-wall in the entryway, I knew what had happened. Tiny, dotted footprints covered every surface in the kitchen, making my counters look like the world's tiniest Santa clause had come early. In the pile of flour on the floor, the small prints continued, dragging together to form capital letters that read "BEWARE THE MERMAN."

Fucking fairies.

I slid my foot through it just as Leith appeared over my shoulder, wiping away the words.

"Rats," I said, shrugging. "Downside to living in a charming historical building. I'll deal with it later. Would you like a beer?"

"Those are some big rats if they can haul a five-pound bag of flour off the shelf in the cabinet."

"If not a beer, maybe you'd like to see the bedroom?"

"Is that where you keep the baseball bat for clubbing your mega-rats?"

"Ugh, fine, you caught me," I threw an exaggerated eye roll and tried to come up with something ridiculous. "Fairies broke into my kitchen to send me a message using flour. Are we done now?"

Holy shit. That was not ridiculous, that was the truth. And it just popped out of my mouth like I ran around telling people my secrets all the time. I tried not to look startled as Leith cracked a grin. He looped an arm around my waist and pulled me into him.

"I knew there was something magical about you, Caoimhe Ryan." I could not tell, based solely on his smile and the way he was looking at me, if he knew I *wasn't* joking.

For the first time in my life, I felt something warm and comfortable join the anxious whispers on continual loop in my mind—something that said Leith knowing the truth might not lead to my eventual ruin.

Maybe, it said. *Just maybe.*

That was too much to manage right then, pressed against Leith and the full force of his smile. I shoved the thought down, dismissing the voice, and pulled Leith's mouth down to mine, tangling us in the kind of breathless kiss that makes everything else fade away to white noise.

It worked like a charm—too well, even, for something magical to replicate. If I wasn't careful, I could get addicted to this kind of blissful abyss.

Slowly, Leith pressed into the kiss harder, until my back met the kitchen counter. He slid his hands down the length of my body until they found my thighs, circling around to cup the backs.

"Up," he said, voice barely more than a low purr, and I found myself airborne as he lifted me bodily onto the counter. I wrapped my legs around his waist and pulled him into me, feeling how hard he was through his jeans. I scooted myself forward, eagerly grinding against his length and we both let out a low moan.

"I have a bedroom," I gasped as Leith moved his attention to my neck, nipping lightly before finding the tender place at the base and biting.

"It's rude to eat in bed," he said, sliding those deliciously calloused hands under my shirt and along the length of my back. I let him hook his thumbs along the hem of my shirt and pull it up and over.

My nipples immediately strained beneath my bra, desperate for attention. I was hot and wet in my jeans. I couldn't remember the last time I was this turned on.

Leith deftly unhooked my bra, not giving me time to shiver in the chilly kitchen as he covered each breast with a warm rough hand. I arched into his touch, greedy for it after so many teasing, brief moments. I wanted to feel him on every part of me the way I felt his thumb on my hand.

He pinched and rolled one nipple. I saw sparks, nearly slipping off the counter. He caught me with the other hand, holding me in place at the hip and grinding into me harder on the counter. We were both breathless and desperate, Leith angling his mouth down and catching my nipple lightly with his teeth. I threw my head back in the ecstasy of the soft pain and tried to muffle the scream that wanted to rip through my throat.

If Pete knocked on my door and interrupted us, I would have to murder him on the spot.

I reached for Leith's pants but he caught my hands, intertwining our fingers and pressing them back to the counter while he kissed me again. I was stunned by the sudden intimacy of the gesture, the need for soft contact in the heat of the moment. Everything stilled within me and I forgot for a moment my singing nerves and burning skin, how desperately I sought release between my legs.

For just that moment, nothing else existed but the warmth and comfort of kissing Leith. And then he shifted against me and his t-shirt against my exposed nipples made me catch my breath, slamming me back into my body from where I'd been floating above it.

He dipped his head toward my breasts again and I stopped him, catching his jaw in my hands and pulling him back up toward me.

He squinted, concerned, and pulled away.

"Everything okay?"

"Too okay," I said, fully aware I was breathing like I'd run a marathon. "We're going to start a fire in here if we don't take off our pants."

"I've never had anyone stop me because I was doing too good of a job," he grinned at me, a dangerous glint in his eye. I flushed as his gaze landed heavily on me, roving over every part like I desperately needed his hands and mouth to do.

"There's a first time for everything," I said, closing the space between us and sliding my arms around his neck. "Now would you please help a girl finish before your masterpiece is overworked?"

Small lines appeared between his brows and he seemed to be studying me carefully.

"Let me see," he said thoughtfully running his hands down my bare back. I leaned my head on his shoulder, trying to take in the touch and not cry at the sudden lancing flush of heat that was building further in my core. "Light and shading are realistic."

He slid his fingers lightly in the waistband of my pants and I closed my eyes, focusing only on his satisfying touch on skin that had been waiting its turn. He undid my pants and I lifted myself up to help him pull them off.

"Figure is—" here, he paused, pulling away and taking me in with a fresh heat and hunger, deeper and sharper than before. His eyes were dark, like thunderclouds, and a muscle twitched in his jaw. "—perfection," he breathed.

He stepped back to the counter kissing me in the same breathless way, then guided me gently so that I was laying down. I felt exposed and a small trill of panic rose up in my chest, but then he was kissing my hips, running warm hands over my thighs and pulling my underwear off.

Nothing else mattered but his mouth placing small bites and kisses up and down the length of my thighs. There was no other concern on this planet than how soon he was going to put his mouth on me. I lifted up at the waist, not caring if he thought I was pushy.

I was on fire and I needed to be smothered immediately.

He pressed his hand flat on my stomach, pushing me back to the counter and pinning me there.

"The setting leaves a little to be desired but it is certainly imaginative," he said. "Fairies and all."

"Fuck the fairies," I whined. "Fuck me." I was writhing beneath his hand on the counter. I'd never wanted someone to fuck me so badly. What was he *doing* to me?

He knelt down, bringing his broad shoulders level with the counter and my pussy, dangling one leg over his shoulder, and pushing the other up so that it rested more securely on the counter.

"I suppose the work can be finished, for now," he whispered between my legs and I nearly shot off the counter with need.

I tangled my fingers in his hair and gave a tug.

"Please, Leith." Was it rude to smash a man's face with your vagina on the first date? I was struggling and straining beneath his hands, but he had me in place and I wasn't going anywhere.

"Say it again," his breath was hot against me and I clenched like the air alone could satisfy me.

"Say what?"

"My name."

"Leith," I said as if it was a spell, full of intention and desire.

He groaned, deep and low, the vibration humming through me.

"Leith," I said again, then repeated his name, my voice getting rougher and rougher with desperation until finally his mouth was on me, licking up my folds with expert precision and his name became a fumbled, high-pitched moan.

He ate like a man starved and I was a plate to be cleaned. He licked up and round my clit, stopping to suck and nibble on it delicately. I arched into his mouth, letting go of his hair to slam my hands on the counter for balance. White hot pinpoints of light danced in my vision and I was chasing release.

I heard a zipper from below the counter and Leith groaned against my pussy again, sending that delicious vibration up through me. I was glad I wouldn't finish alone but I was a little disappointed at not getting to see his dick.

Leith led me up, and up, nearing climax as he licked and sucked, working his fingers into me, pressing them wide against my clenching need. I rode his hand to release as he continued to lick my clit in circles, coming in a shower of blinding sparks in my vision. I cried out, clenching one hand on Leith's shoulder, slamming the other on the counter hard enough to sting.

I laid back, spent, and closed my eyes, letting my breathing slow as I came back down to earth.

When I opened my eyes again, Leith was leaning across the counter, over me, one hand cupping my face and tracing my cheek with his thumb. He was looking at me directly, must've been looking at me while I was coming down.

For just a moment, I let myself imagine a life where I was completely honest with someone with no constraints or consequences. I tried to pretend that Leith looking down at me, eyes soft and hazy, was not inspiring a rising panic in my chest, that my mind had not automatically kicked into protection mode now that the sex was over and the tension was gone.

For just a moment, I tried to pretend there was no need for protection.

Maybe, that warm voice said again, quickly overridden by the anxious whispers chanting *too close too close too close* as if the rhythm alone could banish him.

This was it. This was what it always was.

He'd just given me the best orgasm I'd had in years, so naturally it was time to kick him out and never see him again.

Except he's your client.

"Here," Leith said, finally breaking the silence. He slid an arm under my shoulders and carefully helped me sit up. I saw stars from the sudden change and had to steady myself. I realized I couldn't feel my legs and I was terrified of falling over naked in front of him.

"I'll probably need a minute or two here," I said. "You don't have to wait." I noticed he was zipped and tucked back in, all put back together like he hadn't just entirely disassembled a woman on her kitchen counter.

"I won't strand you up there," he said. "If I did my job right, your legs won't work for a while."

"You got me there," I gave him a half smile.

"If you'd let me," he opened his arms wide and made a scooping motion.

"Oh, like a damsel in distress?" I put the back of my hand to my head dramatically.

"Like a queen who's lost a shoe," he said, arms still out.

"When you put it that way, who am I to refuse?"

He lifted me bodily off the counter and I giggled despite myself, kicking my feet out dramatically. He dropped me swiftly but carefully into my bed with a satisfying flounce and leaned down to kiss me once, soft and simple.

"Goodnight, Caoimhe," he said. I was flooded simultaneously with relief and disappointment at the thought of him leaving. "I hope to see you again—outside of work."

"I hope you see me again, too." But there were so many other hopes I was holding. *I hope I don't fuck this up. I hope you aren't a merman. I hope you don't run away when you learn the truth. I hope you don't use me. I hope Nan is wrong.*

My bed was soft and warm and my body was exhausted. I let my eyes drift closed as I felt Leith's weight leave the bed, as I heard his quiet footsteps pad through the apartment and the final latch click on the door.

I slipped into sleep, full of hope.

12

Leith

"Do you think we could be something?"

It was a dirty trick to get a woman to confess something before I had to, and I tried to justify it to myself the next morning. I hadn't known, then, if Caoimhe was as unusual as I suspected. And I wasn't going to reveal myself—and Will—on a first date, no matter how stunning and clever and enchanting the woman was.

Of course, as soon as we saw the mess in her kitchen, I knew *for sure* she was one of us. No one else was so desperate to dismiss the clear image of tiny footprints and writing all over their kitchen unless they were trying to distract someone else from it. And the fact that she jumped straight from rats to fairies was a dead giveaway—no raccoons or possums, no jealous ex, no Pete with poor boundaries.

It was fucking fairies.

I didn't know if she fully understood what I was saying to her when I told her I knew there was magic in her. I resolved to clarify as soon as I could. But first, I had to get through my initial consultation with Tony the emotion coach.

My phone stared back at me from the coffee table, daring me to check it one more time. It was one minute until our call time. Tony would call me, he said. The phone would ring. I didn't need to keep picking it up and checking the screen.

I thought about Caoimhe's drowsy form last night, sprawled across her bed, satiated.

It wasn't Tony's call I was waiting for and every other part of myself knew it.

"Slow down," I muttered to myself just as the screen lit up and I lunged forward to answer like a man waiting on bad news.

"Leith! How are you, man?" His voice was bright and full of Boston, all soft vowels and dropped hard consonants. "I'm glad we could sync up. It's not wicked early for you, is it?"

I shook my head then realized he couldn't see me. "It's alright," I said.

"Good, good. So Caoimhe sent you, huh? What a great girl, right?"

I nodded but he continued on anyway.

"She's a real one," he said. "Sends me some of my best clients. So, tell me what's going on. Why are you looking into coaching?"

"I threw someone off a boat," I answered, feeling the thud of the truth hit the air.

"He probably deserved it." I could hear Tony shrug. "But it's not about who deserved what or who shouldn't have done this or that. It's about how we recognize, acknowledge, and give permission to our emotions."

Tony walked me through what a basic coaching plan would include—I could text him throughout the day when "big emotions" came up to talk through how to process them in a productive way and we'd have calls once a week to recap how I thought things were going. I wasn't sure what I'd text him about now that I was swimming again. The ocean soothed all the things that had led to my outburst the other day. But I didn't want to let Caoimhe down, even if it meant telling this stranger about my weekly emotional state.

"I'll work out the rate with Caoimhe and your boss, don't worry about that."

"Are you sure?"

"Of course! C and I go way back, I'm always happy to help her clients out."

A pang of jealousy twitched within me and I tucked it away. There was so much I didn't know about Caoimhe, of course she had other relationships regardless of their nature.

We said our goodbyes and I agreed to text Tony starting that afternoon.

It was early yet for me to show up at the docks, and my head was whirling from the past twenty-four hours. I decided to risk a swim.

There was a spot along the harbor, not far from Mister Flipper, where no one but a few burnt-out deckhands ever passed through. If I dipped into the water and didn't reappear, they'd either chalk it up to the drugs or assume I wanted to be left alone regardless. It wasn't an elegant solution—I would still have to get out of the water again—but it worked for now since I didn't want to wait for nightfall.

I slipped on my jacket, taking a deep breath as the sound of Caoimhe saying my name echoed through me. My cock twitched in my jeans and I thought about masturbating instead of swimming horny.

Maybe the cold water would be enough to shock me back to my senses.

At the docks, I turned left instead of my usual right, heading further down to where a few stray fishing boats were still anchored, rocking lightly in the current. I passed a few men in coveralls and rubber boots, exchanging a quick nod before continuing. This was not the part of the docks that dabbled in small talk or traded on customer service quality. And if I kept walking with my shoulders back and my steps even, no one would ask what I was doing there—even if I clearly wasn't a fisherman.

I found my spot blessedly empty, the sad, rusted boat usually tied there was absent, with no deckhands to navigate around. I slipped out of my clothes, leaving them in an empty barrel nearby and lowered myself into the water, avoiding any loud splashing. The last thing I needed was someone thinking a seal or sea lion had gotten lost.

Under the water, I kicked off the support beam of the dock launching myself out further into the harbor, relishing the change that came over me as I felt my tail and dorsal fin pull together from my body. The water was cool and quiet, the current whispering its usual call to the open ocean. Today, I allowed it to lure me away, swimming further and further away from Boston and out past the small islands that marked the entrance to the Atlantic.

The water was colder here, darker and wilder. I felt primal things surfacing within me, my more animalistic urges taking control. Microscopic prey caught the sun as my eyes adjusted, setting the world around me alight with tiny sparks of flickering life. I wasn't kidding when I told Will I didn't feed in my mershark form. I still had a human-like mouth, which made trying to filter feed like my whale shark ancestors impossible. Besides, I'd discovered apples, cantaloupe, watermelon, peaches—fresh fruit was the land dweller gift that never stopped giving.

I swam on, following a school of silver fish, zigzagging lazily through them, enjoying the rush of the water they kicked up around us. But still, there beat a need within my pulse that was not satiated by my transformation—a need that spoke of dangerous things for my human counterparts if I couldn't find a way to satiate it.

The problem was there were no other whale sharks in the Boston harbor. We were normally warm-water people, preferring the tropical waters of reefs and islands to the harsh chill of the Atlantic.

For the first time since I lost my temper, since I met Caoimhe, since my world seemed to have been tilted off its access, I thought of Lisa.

I thought she'd be my mate after I met her in the harbor one night, both of us cautiously circling one another under the waves. After Onda, I'd thought Will and I would be the only merfolk on the East Coast, everyone else warned off by the dense human population. But there Lisa had been, all sleek grey curves and sharp teeth.

Our relationship moved faster than her fins cutting the water. One moment she was in the ocean and the next she was in my bed. But she hated being around humans, resented me dragging her from the water for more than a day at a time. She insisted I was denying my true self, and that sooner or later, when humans found me out, I'd go the same way as Onda—or worse.

It was Lisa's voice that haunted me when I found myself in particularly dangerous human interactions. It was Lisa's voice that day on the boat, echoing through my mind with the last thing she'd said to me before leaving Boston permanently.

"You love those mortals but wait until they learn about your true nature—wait until they see you've got teeth."

But that hadn't been everything.

"You are not a beautiful, powerful thing to them," she'd continued, standing in the doorway to my apartment. "You're a monster. A danger. Something to be avoided. They will find out what you are and they will hunt you down. Don't be deluded by a few soft songs and watercolors."

She turned to go, glancing over her shoulder at me one last time before disappearing from my life forever.

"And they will find out, Leith. It is only a matter of time."

I'd abstained from swimming after that. I wanted to prove her wrong. I wanted to prove to myself that I could contain my true nature and stay in this place that was becoming my home. Will did it. Kelly did it. I could, too.

Then there was Julie. Then there was the boat incident.

Now there was Caoimhe.

Caoimhe inspired something deep within me to spring to life, something that Lisa had never triggered—that no one had ever triggered.

I didn't know enough about her yet to risk revealing myself. And even then, there was no guarantee she could mate successfully with me. I didn't exactly have the usual number of appendages that humanoid women—Fae retinue or not—were used to. I didn't want to win her over just to chase her away with my more monstrous features. Short of crawling into an aquarium tank for a quick fuck, I would have to swim south for the winter in search of another whale shark to mate with or be plagued continuously by the heat in my blood.

I already knew there was no number of texts to Tony that could help me process the instinctual sense in my core that Caoimhe was my mate. How would I explain to him that it wasn't just emotion, but nature at work? An almost blinding animalistic need that could make me do stupid things in the name of release?

I looped one of the islands at the mouth of the bay, trying to make sense of my situation while letting my shark-half enjoy the speed of whipping through the water carelessly.

There was always the option of paying for relief and discretion. Will had suggested it jokingly on more than one occasion but I knew it was a possibility. Enough cash on the table and anyone wouldn't blink twice at having an extra dick.

But that would run the risk of hurting Caoimhe. I was already too attached to her despite our limited time together, the suggestion of being with someone else made my heart ache.

And more than anything—beyond my instincts, beyond my base needs and urges—I wanted it to be with Caoimhe. I wanted *her*.

I would find a way, even if it meant suffering until the end.

FOR IMMEDIATE RELEASE FROM MISTER FLIPPER

Boston, MA. Mister Flipper is thrilled to announce their partnership with local mental health service Very Well Boston to provide improved services and care to their employees.

The announcement comes after the unfortunate incident between a tour boat operator and a guest wherein an altercation escalated to physical action. Mister Flipper is dedicated to the safety and wellness of all persons aboard their tours and believe that equipping their employees with strong tools for regulation and de-escalation are critical to improved safety going forward.

"Mister Flipper has been around since I was a kid," says Anthony d'Alessi, CEO of Very Well Boston and certified emotions coach. "I'm honored that a legacy company is willing to explore new ways of operating with us. It speaks to their integrity as a member of Boston's small business community as well as an employer. I believe wonderful things will come of this partnership for all involved."

"We want our team to have the best possible resources every time they're out on the water," says Kelly Nerida, co-founder and head operations manager of Mister Flipper. "And that means they're emotionally equipped as well, even if that's not the first thing anyone thinks of when they think 'tour boat.'"

In addition to internal mental health services, Very Well Boston and Mister Flipper will be partnering to produce a community appreciation carnival, with free games and food for all who wish to attend. Dates and times to be announced.

13

Caoimhe

I knocked again on Will's door and waited, arms crossed in my best silk blouse. I tapped a heeled foot against the wooden landing. I had a meeting with Mirabel and the Hollywood agent to discuss a potential film adaptation of her debut novel but first I needed to clear my latest anxiety.

Will finally cracked the door open, blinking in the morning light. He smelled of cigarettes and a late night.

"Are you a merman?" I asked.

He blinked again and squinted. "Is that what you're into?"

"Don't be gross," I said, pushing against the door and shoving my way into the apartment. Will let me, dropping his arms to his side to make room. He still hadn't unpacked, and cardboard boxes towered in various corners. His kitchen had a few old takeout containers sitting on the counter and I noticed two pairs of chopsticks sitting by the sink. Toward the back of the apartment, I could see the bedroom door was closed.

"Answer the question," I said, my nerves humming and every part of me hoping against all odds that I was wrong, that the fairy tail was wrong.

"If I am?" He reached a hand to his mouth instinctually, then seemed to be confused by the lack of cigarette dangling from it. "You gonna have Pete kick me out?"

I shook my head. "You can be my neighbor, but you cannot prey on my best friend. If you're a merman, you have to break up with Evelyn."

"Then I'm not a merman." He shrugged as if that ended the conversation, then fixed me with a stare, daring me to pick the thread back up.

I took it.

"*If* you are a merman," I stepped forward, recrossing my arms and letting my shoulders settle back. He didn't move but I noticed his eyes grow wide. "And *if* that hurts Eve in some way, I will make sure you are in pain for the rest of your life."

"You promise?" He arched an eyebrow at me suggestively.

"I promise, Will Burleigh."

"You're not her keeper," he said, leaning into my threatening stance. "She can make her own decisions, 'dangerous' or not."

I narrowed my eyes, taking him in. "You look like you eat takeout more than human women," I whispered.

"Is that supposed to be an insult?" he whispered back.

It was. And I was doing a bad job of trying to intimidate the truth out of my neighbor. I heaved a sigh and threw my hands in the air.

"Fine! Don't tell me." I let my arms drop. "Keep your secret."

"It's not a secret if you've figured it out." I froze. Will's face was stone still and he seemed to be waiting for my response.

"You're something else."

"You know," I breathed.

"I suspect," he said. "Should I know?"

I shook my head and tried not to let fear push me out the door, out of the building, out of this topsy-turvy world I'd stepped into.

"I don't know anymore," I said more to myself than to Will.

"It's okay to trust people sometimes," Will offered. "Everyone has secrets, I think you'll find more support than you know."

I wanted to believe him, wanted to let go of all the work it took to keep myself buried. I wanted to know what it felt like to be free from fear and suspicion, to trust someone without having to verify their identity—without needing to know they wouldn't hurt me.

"Like they did your father."

I started to shake despite myself and decided it was time to go. I turned to leave, not even offering a goodbye but Will's voice followed me down the stairs.

"You can trust Leith."

God, I wanted to.

***

The meeting with Mirabel passed in a blur. I barely registered any of the conversation, but it seemed my work was done for me when the agent agreed to some of Mirabel's bigger requests—control over adaptation, rights and royalties, and, incredibly, the final say on casting the leads.

"Can you believe how lucky we got?" She asked, gleefully wrapping my hands in the tinkling silver of her wrists.

"I can't!" I exclaimed.

I could.

I decided I needed the rest of the day off to clear my head. Flashes of Leith between my legs, of saying his name at the peak of climax, were mixed with Will's shark-like smile, his promise to trust them.

Everything felt like it was moving too fast and yet nothing had changed. I was still fielding calls from my grandmother, still clacking home across the cobblestones to my apartment, still letting my ancestral charm luck debut artists into the chances of a lifetime.

So why did it feel like I was suddenly on another planet?

Coming down my street, I recognized a familiar head of blindingly blonde curls sitting on my front stoop. I risked a broken ankle to run down the sidewalk, clearing the distance between us in a few breathless seconds.

"Mom!" I shrieked, letting her scoop me into a comforting hug that smelled of fresh grass, sunbaked dirt, and something bright, like clean laundry. I pulled away to get a better look at her. We had the same unruly hair, the same bright eyes. I had Dad's nose and sharp tongue but just about everything else came from my mom. She was a little more tanned and wrinkled than the last time I'd seen her over a year ago, clear evidence of her time abroad.

She kissed my cheek and squeezed my shoulders. "Are you hungry?" she asked, her lilting accent barely there even after all these years.

"Always," I said.

After dashing up to change my shoes, we headed off, arm in arm, in search of sandwiches. My mom had been around the world and back, she liked to say, and few places had a good turkey sandwich like the American East Coast.

We settled in a park with a can of Coke between us, sandwiches clutched in eager hands.

"So, Caoimhe, dearest, we have to talk," she said, taking a bite and chewing thoughtfully. I waited, unsure what was coming. The last time she'd started a conversation that way it had been to announce she was taking off to travel for an unknown amount of time. After Dad died, she'd drifted from country to country, seeking solace in strange places. "I came back because your grandmother called me, absolutely frantic."

I rolled my eyes out of habit before catching Mom's glare and apologizing around a mouthful of sandwich.

"We've discussed that attitude, missy," she said, arching her eyebrows. "We respect our elders in this family, even if we disagree with them."

"You came all this way to lecture me on my manners?"

"I came all this way because I was told you were getting involved with a merman."

"No, that's my best friend," I said automatically. Mom dropped her sandwich back onto the paper bag it had been wrapped in, wiping her hands free of stray lettuce.

"That's not funny, Caoimhe."

"It's not meant to be." When Mom didn't say anything more, I continued. "I *may* have encountered a merman, but I'm not involved with him directly. He's my neighbor and my best friend might be seeing him."

"That's not what Violet reported back."

Realization dawned like feeling returning to a sleeping limb.

"*You* hired the fairy tail."

"You didn't expect me to leave my only child in another country and not have *someone* keep an eye on you?"

"I did, actually. I thought Nan hired them."

"She probably has her own." Mom shrugged. "You're precious cargo, dearest, espccially in this crowd."

Well, that explained my fairy problem.

"Caoimhe, I hate to say it, but it may be time to go home."

I stared. Mom refused my entire life to return to Ireland. She insisted we were fine among the humans, that Boston was more our home than anywhere else. Even after Dad was found out, even after we lost him, she dug in further, telling Nan in no uncertain terms where she could stick her demands.

Mom was the reason I was so sure Boston was home, that I was so sure this was where I belonged and where my heart was.

"Where is this coming from?"

Mom looked down at her hands, twisting them together. She refused to make eye contact and I waited for her to answer.

"I was found out," she said. "In Brazil. I made it out alive, but only barely. This world is getting too dangerous for folk like us."

She looked up at me, placing one hand on mine and squeezing it. Her face was desperate, full of fear. I'd never seen her like this.

"I won't be able to live with myself if I lost my husband to humans and my daughter to merfolk," she said. "And I won't be taken either. We should go where we'll be protected, where we'll be powerful."

I shook my head, disbelief coursing through me and threatening to knock me off my seat.

"Take some time and think about it," she said. "I'll be in town a few days to get the last of my things and start planning the trip back."

"If I don't go with you, what happens?" I asked.

"You'll always be my girl," she said, but I saw a heavy sadness stretch across her face. It was nearly enough to force my hand right then. But I knew my mom didn't want that for me. She wanted me to be happy—wherever that was.

We sat in silence for a few minutes, letting the fall breeze whisper above us.

"Is it possible to trust humans?" I didn't look at her, staring instead at the dappled light streaming through the leaves. They'd turn red and brown and gold soon, setting each tree alight with an ever-burning fire.

"There is magic in all things, Caoimhe," she answered. "Even humans."

That wasn't *really* an answer, but it might be the most I got given her current fears.

"But it is a greater risk to seek it," she continued.

I glanced over to see she was gazing out across the park. The lines around her eyes had deepened, and there were fresh wrinkles along her forehead and jaw. I knew we weren't immortal, but it was as if Dad's absence had aged her more than any years that passed.

I tried not to think too much about that night. It had only been two years, but still the memories felt faded—dampened by the need to keep living in the face of death.

Dad had trusted his best friend, John, with his true identity. They'd been drinking together, and John shared that he was knee-deep in debt to a loan shark with a mean streak. Dad, wanting to help, told John who and what we were, but worse, he told him what we could do. John immediately demanded Dad give him gold. When he explained that wasn't possible—there was never any gold—John lost it and shot him at close range.

I thought about the flashing lights through our window that night when the cops came with the news. I'd vowed to never tell a human the truth about myself.

The breeze shifted and the smell of salt was light in the air, pulling my thoughts with it to Leith and his gentle gaze, his careful calloused hands.

"Do you think we could be something?"

All this hiding, the constant fear, the smothering of myself under layers of vague answers and expert subject changes. I couldn't really connect with anyone, leaving my bed cold and my phone silent. I even lied to Evelyn. Every day. It was exhausting. I looked again at the lines around Mom's eyes, reaching a hand up to my own cheeks and tracing the skin there.

How much longer could I carry on like this? And what toll would it take?

The alternative stunk of airplanes and regret. I could already see myself crying on the plane next to Mom as we left behind the only home I'd ever known. A sharp pain in my heart told me immediately that leaving wasn't the answer. Which left only one alternative.

"I think I need to risk it," I said.

Mom closed her eyes, a tear sliding down her cheek, and nodded. "I know, sweet girl," she said. "I know."

14

Leith

"What do you think about a balloon dart game?" Kelly held the phone receiver down from her mouth and whispered to us across the office.

Will nodded. I shook my head. Kelly rolled her eyes.

"Bean bag toss then?"

Will shook his head. I nodded.

"Gods below and above, get out. You're both useless." She waved her arms and went back to talking to the carnival game rentals on the phone. Caoimhe had already spoken to Tony and his company agreed to not only co-sponsor our event, but to do it this upcoming weekend.

"The quicker we move, the sooner you can stop being Dunk Man," Kelly explained. I hated receiving news of Caoimhe second-hand even if it was a side of the business I had nothing to do with. I still couldn't quell the jealousy I felt over her "history" with Tony—whatever it was.

Incredibly, our two p.m. tour was booked solid for the first time all summer. I felt a rising dread as I passed the queue to board and several young men with their phones aimed at me started chanting "Dunk Man! Dunk Man! Dunk Man!" My suspicions were confirmed when someone at the head of the line yelled "Dunk me next!"

"You don't have to do this," Will said to me, leaning in to shield me from the crowd.

"You can't run the boat alone and Kel has her hands full. It'll be fine."

"Maybe stay at the helm then."

Once everyone boarded and figured out Dunk Man wouldn't be making an appearance, the crowd quieted down—although some younger guests remained restless and disinterested. I heard a few stray, "Where's Dunk Man," calls from up within the steering station but Will quickly started talking into the mic about jellyfish penises and that seemed to distract them.

After returning to the dock, I waited longer than usual until Will poked his head in the door.

"All clear, Dunk Man."

"Don't," I growled.

"I would have more sympathy for you but you got yourself into this mess."

"Do you wanna run the four p.m. alone?"

"I'll run everything alone, baby, I'm a rogue wolf." He howled in a ridiculous dramatic stance, arms spread wide, back arched, lips pushed up.

I smiled despite myself. Will was like that, always twirling away from the serious into something silly. At least he used to be before he started drinking so heavily.

Although…

"Are you sober?"

"That's rude," he sniffed. "I'm working, of course I'm sober."

"You seem…" I squinted at him letting the rest of the thought drop off. He shrugged and turned to do a quick cleanup of the deck between tours. I followed, trying to place what it was that seemed different that day.

"Handsome? Clever? Talented?" Will finished for me, grinning. "Why thank you, Leith, but you know you and I could never be. I already have both my own penises competing with each other, I don't think I could handle two new challengers in the arena."

"Happy." There it was. Will, always charming and quick-witted, was also miserable, smoking a cigarette or chugging a bottle. Yet here he was, smiling while sober and I hadn't seen him smoke since we got to the office.

Will's face dropped to something softer, and the usual shark-like grin turned thoughtful. "I think I am," he said. He looked up at me through his dark hair. "I went for a swim last night."

I tripped over a row of seats, banging my thigh against the metal. "You *what*."

"It was time," he said. "I told you I'd do it when I was ready."

"No you didn't." He told me to fuck off or changed the subject entirely.

"Well, what I *meant* was I would do it when I was ready. A real friend would know that, obviously." He gestured to yet another line-up of teens with phones down on the dock. "You should get back up in that steering station before they start chanting again."

I heaved a sigh and returned to the helm, drumming my fingers against the metal wheel. Something was different about Will—something had shifted in the last week. And it was big enough that he was avoiding telling me.

I racked my brain, trying to think of what I'd missed. It felt like I had only barely resurfaced from a deep dive into chaos. With losing my temper, seeing Caoimhe, and running tours, the rest of my life felt like a distant planet—including my best friend.

Watching the guests begin to board, I resolved to take Will out after work and catch up.

***

Caoimhe: *Can we talk please? Soon?*

Caoimhe: *Shit, that sounds ominous. It's good, I promise.*

Caoimhe: *Well I think it's good.*

Caoimhe: *Hello?*

"Whatever you did on that date has her *hooked*, dude," Will said around a mouthful of ice cream, leaning over my shoulder.

I shrugged him off and typed out a response. My phone had been going off in my pocket while Will and I ordered our after-work sundaes. I'd decided against offering him a beer because I wanted to encourage his continued sober streak.

Leith: *With Will. I can meet you after.*

"Add a smiley face. You text like you're pissed off."

"No," I turned to shield my phone with my body and then sent a quick smiley face.

Caoimhe: *Great, just come to my place whenever you're free.*

Two nights in a row. My heart was thudding in my chest and my pants suddenly felt incredibly tight. Could I survive two nights in a row with this woman? Maybe if we stayed out of the kitchen. And away from the couch. Definitely not in the bedroom.

Flashes of fucking Caoimhe on her floor, the cheap carpet pebbling my knees and palms as she cried out made me drop my spoon.

"Dude," Will grinned at me, chocolate sauce smeared along his chin like a toddler. "Have you not hooked up with her yet?"

"We have."

"You look like a seal who just remembered the best fish they ever ate."

"I do *not* look like a fucking seal." I pointed my spoon at him. "*You* look like a seal with all that shit on your face."

"So it was good," he said, wiping his face.

"You tell *me* what's good," I said, giving Will a taste of his own medicine. "What has you dancing around like life is sunshine and rainbows?"

"Not all of us enjoy competitive brooding," he said. "Can't I just be upbeat?"

"No."

Will looked down at his half-eaten sundae and then out the window, that same softness settling into his normally jagged features.

"I think it's Evelyn," he said.

"The human woman Kelly told you not to date."

"We all knew I wasn't going to listen to her, that doesn't matter," he said. "Eve does something to me. She doesn't care what anyone thinks, she goes for what she wants—she's kinda like a shark in that way."

I was going to fall out of my seat.

"You're in love," I said.

Will turned back to me, that same rounded smile from before settled into his face. It made him look older, comfortable—not like his usual restless self.

"I might be," he said. "I might be in love with a human woman."

"So...she knows," I said. She had to know.

"Well..." Will's face dropped and he set his spoon down.

"You've had sex how could she *not* know?"

"Well." Will looked up at me meaningfully.

"No way." Eve and Will were all over each other every opportunity they had. They were practically screaming to strangers about how they were going to fuck one another in crude, ridiculous ways. But they hadn't?

Will shrugged. "It hasn't been right."

"Get out." I pointed to the door. "I don't know who you are but give me back Will Burleigh."

"I can move slow! You don't have the market cornered on old-school romance, Mister Painter Man."

"You have to tell her," I said, fully aware that I wasn't just talking about Will anymore.

"I can't," he said. "I can't lose her."

"Maybe you won't," I said. "She's friends with Caoimhe, right? She has to have noticed all the weird shit that happens to her."

Will looked at me, skeptical, before shoving a large bite of half-melted ice cream into his mouth.

"I will if you will," I said finally, feeling my whole body tense at the very thought.

"No, I Will, you Leith."

"I'm serious."

"I know." Will reached across the table and offered me a hand. I took it and shook. We both looked grim, as if we'd made a murderous pact over ice cream and not promised to tell the women we loved the truth about who we were.

And there it was, I realized, still holding Will's hand. Rising unbidden through all the other chaos, all the other fears and worries about what would happen next—love.

"I'm not gonna kiss you," Will said. "So you should let go of my hand and stop looking at me like that."

I pulled his hand hard across the table, launching him forward and gave him a quick kiss on the forehead.

"Don't deny our love," I said, standing up.

"Ew cooties!" he hollered after me as I threw him a wave and left the ice cream shop.

I needed to see Caoimhe—before I lost the guts to do what I'd promised just then. Before I lost the guts to tell her the truth.

Fighting the urge to launch myself into the ocean and never return, I turned up the street, away from the harbor, and headed toward her building.

15

Caoimhe

"I'm a leprechaun."

He was going to laugh at me.

I leaned against my bathroom sink, looking up at my miserable face in the mirror.

"I have magical powers."

Nope that also fell flat.

"I'm lucky and so are you." Even with the finger guns that one wasn't funny.

"How the hell am I going to do this?" I asked the empty room. I could just *not* tell him. I could just *not* tell anyone. My old way of life reared its head, inviting me into the comfort of known stress, of known dangers and risks.

Maybe Leith would sweep into the apartment, wrap me in his arms, and refuse to allow me to speak until he'd had his way with me. Then at least I could claim I was too distracted to talk.

But no. As much as the heat between my legs loved that option, my gut told me Leith would want to know what was on my mind first.

"Of course he's sensitive. The bastard." I smacked my sink and walked away, out into the living room where I'd been pacing for the last hour since texting him. For the millionth time, I chided myself for trying to play it cool instead of demanding he come over immediately—or at least tell me when he was on his way.

Was the path I'd worn in the carpet obvious or was my mind playing tricks on me?

I grabbed a beer from the fridge and took a deep gulp, relishing the cold carbonation as it ripped down my throat.

I could do this. I just told Mom I was going to do this. She was worried. Of course she was worried. She told me she wouldn't try to stop me—something about not wanting to repeat the sins of her mother. She trusted me. So I should trust me.

Right?

"This is a massive mistake," I whispered. A bell chimed from the air and I groaned. The fairy tail, Violet, appeared a few inches from my face, her multi-faceted eyes catching both the sunset outside and the fluorescent kitchen lights.

"What do *you* want?" I spit out, taking another sip of beer.

"Dame Ryan requests your presence at her home."

"Yeah, my mom already talked to me and I told her no."

"It is a matter of grave urgency."

"We both know it's not."

"She told me to say that."

"Alrighty, message received." I tried to wave her off but she dodged my hands in the air.

"There hasn't been a Fae-merfolk alliance in some time," she said, her tiny voice thoughtful.

"We're not allied," I said. "We're—"

A soft knock came at the door.

"—fucked." I waved the fairy away with what I hoped was finality.

"Get out," I hissed. "And tell your friends to stay the hell out of my cabinets."

I opened the door to Leith and my heart leapt into my throat.

"Hi," we both said at the same time. He leaned in to kiss me at the same time I held my arms out for a hug. Then we switched. I heard myself giggle awkwardly and my legs had the sense to move out of the way as I held the door open for him to come in.

"You wanted to talk?" He asked and I could see how high his shoulders were clenched, wanted to reach out and soothe the tight line of his mouth.

"Yes, but don't—"

"Did you have a return message?"

The fairy tail was still hovering in the air, six inches of purple flesh and shimmering dragonfly wings.

I froze, unable to look anywhere but the traitorous magical creature in my living room.

No turning back now.

"I won't be returning," I said. "If Dame Ryan has urgent business to discuss with her granddaughter, she has my number."

The fairy gave me a mock bow and then disappeared with a pop of thin air.

Fucking fairies.

I couldn't decide if I wanted to turn around and face Leith. This was not how I wanted to have this conversation. But I couldn't keep staring at nothing.

Right?

"I knew it."

I whipped around, startled by the shit-eating grin splitting Leith's face from ear to ear. He looked like he'd caught me cheating on a sports bet, not talking to a fairy.

"I *knew* it!" He scooped me up by the waist, whirling us both around and sending my beer sloshing all over the carpet.

"Knew what?" I gasped out.

"Is that your escort to keep you pure for your future husband?"

"*WHAT*? No, my grandmother sends them because I don't answer her billion calls every day—"

"You're not human," he said. "You're not human, you're not promised, and it's perfect!"

"What are you talking about?" I patted his shoulder and wiggled my feet, wanting down. He set me down, but didn't let go, keeping me pressed into his chest.

"It sounds stupid if I say it," He murmured.

"I know how that goes," I said. Everything felt sideways and my heart was going to leap out of my chest. Fear was pounding through my veins but something stronger held my feet in place, kept me close to this strange man in front of me.

"Could I show you?" The full force of his gaze was like being swept out to sea. It was suddenly too much, to be caught so vulnerable so suddenly—to be met with the same when I had expected rejection and pain.

"I can't." The words were out before I could stop them. I watched Leith's face fold in and his eyes shutter. I hated myself for letting the fear win, for being overwhelmed in the face of what should've been a wondrous thing.

He'd seen the fairy and not run, not demanded, not panicked. In fact, he'd seen the fairy and known immediately what it was.

Instead, I was the one who was panicking. I needed to clear my head. I needed a do-over. I needed fairy repellent.

"Wait," I said gripping his arms before he could pull away. "Can I have a do-over?"

He looked confused. I led him to the door, nudging him just past the threshold and held my hand out in command. "Wait here, please, just give me one second."

I closed the door, knuckles white on the knob, palm sweating profusely. I braced my other hand against the worn wood, heaving in one deep breath and letting it out slowly. My lungs hurt, like I'd been running uphill, and everywhere I looked was tilted slightly off center. I waited until the room stopped spinning, until I felt firmly rooted to where I was.

In the face of overwhelm, I allowed myself two firm options. I could open the door and lie. I could tell Leith to leave, that it wasn't working out between us and that I never wanted to see him again. I could just ignore that he'd already seen the fairy and pretend I didn't know what he was talking about.

Or I could tell the truth.

"I need to risk it."

I didn't know where Leith had come from, or what it was about him that made him feel like the only safe place to land I had in the entire world, but something deep in my very core told me if I didn't at least chance it with him—if I didn't pry my fears off my heart—I would regret it for the rest of my life.

Suddenly I was tired. I was tired of lying to the people I cared about, like Eve—and Leith. I tried to not let out a sob as the realization swelled up into my throat and settled there, thick and hot.

I didn't want to lie to Leith because I cared about him. It seemed impossible in such a short time, but something greater than either of us was pulling us together.

I knew better than to walk away from a lucky circumstance.

I leaned my head against the door and tried to will my hand to turn the knob, but I was frozen. Anxiety rushed in, gripping my limbs in a vise. I tried not to think of police lights and funerals and Mom's face.

"Caoimhe?" I could barely hear him through the door. But he was still there. Still waiting for me.

"I'm sorry," I said, knowing he probably couldn't hear me. It was too much. Everything all at once like this, it was more than I could handle.

I couldn't do it like I'd told Mom I could. I wanted to back out of this just as much as I wanted to throw open the door. I wanted to pretend I could trust like I'd never been hurt.

But I couldn't. I couldn't open the door and he was going to walk away and I'd never have another chance like this. I'd be trapped in my own personal prison for the rest of my unnaturally long life, wishing I'd just turned the knob.

More footsteps clamored up the steps and I heard murmured conversation on the landing. A familiar set of keys jangled on the other side of the door and knob turned on its own.

Evelyn stepped in, blocking Leith from sight and gently pressing the door closed again behind her.

"You want me to get rid of him?" She looked dangerous, eyes alight, mouth a grim line. Eve would fight that broad-shouldered boatman for me in a heartbeat, all I had to do was say the word.

My heart couldn't take it. I didn't deserve her or her devoted friendship. How could I have lied to her this long?

I started to cry, trying to stifle the sobs that were pressing behind my teeth.

"I'm gonna kill him." She jutted her chin into the air and slid out of her coat—a knee-length black and white geometric thing that she must've swiped from a sample closet somewhere. I noticed then that she was wearing perfume and long chainmail link earrings that dusted her collarbones. She promptly removed them, setting them on the half-wall to my kitchen.

"Did you have a date?" I choked out.

"No, I was at a work thing, some happy hour bullshit. I left early because Will called." She pulled her rings off and flung them around the room, stepping out of her heels.

"Why?"

She shrugged and cracked the knuckles in each hand.

"He does it for me," she said. "That's enough for now."

I didn't have time to react before Eve pulled the door open and swung, catching Leith directly in the jaw.

"Woah!" Will yelled, appearing from nowhere and grabbing Eve's next swing before it could land. "Everybody is going to calm down, *now*."

"He made her cry!" Eve protested, struggling against Will. She slammed a knee into his gut, doubling him over in surprise, before swinging expertly a second time. This time Leith was ready, and he blocked her, throwing his arms up to cover his face.

"Wait, Eve!" I called out but it was no use. She was in murder mode.

I heard thudding footsteps from downstairs and knew Pete was en route. He would at least throw out Leith and Eve since they didn't live here, but I had no idea what kind of trouble I'd be in as a tenant.

I caught Will's eye and gestured frantically downstairs. He nodded, wheezing his way down the stairs to intercept. I braved the landing and looped an arm around Eve's slender waist, hauling her back with my full strength. It wasn't much but it was enough to make her pause her onslaught against Leith's forearms. I made a note to ask him why he was so good at fighting off tiny fashion writers.

"Get in my apartment. Now." I said, pointing firmly to the door. "Both of you."

Eve threw Leith a look that could've melted iron and he slinked behind her into the apartment. I could hear Will downstairs, his laugh ringing up the walls.

When I closed the door behind us, Eve had claimed the couch, sprawling across it defiantly and Leith stood in the kitchen, looking lost.

I turned to them both and everyone started talking at once.

"I have something to—"

"Whatever it is he did—"

"I didn't mean to—"

I held my hands out for silence, grateful when both parties agreed.

"I've been lying to you both," I started.

"You're not a publicist?" Eve sat bolt-right up, eyes wide.

"No! How is that the first thing you thought?"

She shrugged. "You almost never have to do anything, your clients just end up in ridiculously lucky circumstances. I thought maybe you were tied into the mob or something."

"Well, I do have a ridiculous amount of luck, which is—"

"I fucking knew it. You're a mob wife!" Eve was clawing at the back of the couch and any minute she was going to leap over it and onto me.

"I am *not.*" I took a deep breath and looked to Leith. "I'm a leprechaun."

Incredibly, he didn't so much as flinch. He gave me a half-smile and nodded. So he really *did* know. How?

Eve's raucous laughter brought the room back into focus.

"A leprechaun? In Boston? Original, C, I thought you'd come up with a better cover than that." She wiped tears from her eyes and stood up, grabbing her jacket from the back of the couch.

I steadied myself, knowing this was always where this conversation was going to lead. Humans never believed anything until it was staring them square in the face.

"I'll prove it," I said. "But you have to promise not to freak."

"What, you have horns and a tail?"

"What leprechauns have you seen with horns and a tail?" Leith shot from across the kitchen.

I gave them both a look and they fell silent.

I closed my eyes and pulled from deep within myself. It had been a long time since I'd dropped my glamour. I barely had to think about it anymore—it was like remembering to put on mascara in the mornings before leaving the house. But I was surprised to see how quickly I could slip back into that part of myself. I imagined it like taking off a rain parka, like removing a long plastic transparent sheet I'd been wearing for years.

And just like that, I opened my eyes and was barely a foot off the ground. I knew without looking that my ears had grown to a long point, jutting out through my hair, and that everything else about me would have shrunk down to a perfect, delicate miniature.

I scrambled up and over the pile of clothes I lost in my transformation, holding the edge of my blouse over my freshly naked form.

Eve had a hand clamped tightly over her mouth, her eyes bulging to a dramatic size. She was shaking slightly as she knelt in front of me, peering down in disbelief. She blocked Leith from my line of vision, but I could feel his eyes on me nonetheless. I could only hope when I slid back into my glamour he wouldn't be entirely repulsed.

"C," she finally whispered. "You're tiny."

"Not supposed to be more than three fists off the ground, technically," I said. "But we've evolved over time. At least a little."

"You could rob a bank so easily."

"Evelyn Sharp!"

"No, I'm serious! I mean you'd need someone to help you carry out the cash, but you could slide through just about any gap. How mad would you be if I dropped you off at Copley Place tonight?"

I did my best to shoot her a look, knowing it wasn't menacing at all given my size.

Eve giggled, and I saw relief begin to slide across her face.

"Sorry, it's just so weird," she said.

"Just wait," Leith rumbled from above her.

"What does that mean?" she asked.

"It means you should put your girlfriend in your pocket, we're gonna take a trip to the beach." Eve's eyes darted over to Will behind me, standing in the doorway. I must not have locked the door, which, given that I was both tiny and naked, was a dumb move.

"Will, I'm naked!" I shrieked.

"And I need glasses, Duchess, you're safe from my prying eyes."

"Duchess?" Eve looked back to me.

I nodded slowly, unsure how Will knew. "That part is more complicated," I said.

"More complicated than being a leprechaun?"

"Most things are," I laughed. "Nobody look. I'm changing back and it'll take me a second to get dressed."

***

The last tired limbs of the sun were stretching out across the harbor as we made our way through a small park. We were across the bridge from the Mister Flipper docks, a short walk but a decent distance. We followed Will and Leith to the edge of the park that met the water on a sudden drop. They seemed to be looking for something.

"So it takes work to not be tiny, but you're never tiny?" Eve had been drilling me the entire way as if my true form were a titillating date story and not a supernatural phenomenon.

"It's impractical to be a foot tall and live in a human city," I said. "It's overwhelming and exhausting trying to do anything at that size."

"But don't you get tired?"

"I only get tired of having to keep things a secret," I said. "There were so many times I wished I could call you and vent about my grandmother or the fairies breaking shit in my apartment but couldn't. That was the hard part."

Eve squeezed my hand. "No more secrets," she said. "You're my best friend. If you murdered a man I'd be by your side in a heartbeat."

"Please no murder," Will called from ahead of us.

If I closed my eyes for just a second, standing there in against the sunset with Eve nudging my shoulder, I could pretend we were just four friends out for a night together. I could imagine it was a double date that was going well. When it ended, Eve and I would go home to my couch and giggle to each other over the best parts, teasing one another over imagined futures.

But the reality was that we were about to learn something about Will and Leith—something they said could change the way we thought about them. But they hadn't been willing to share more than that.

"You're more likely to murder us!" Eve called back.

"We wouldn't stand a chance against your right hook."

Eve laughed but it was tight, swallowed by the sound of the waves, and I could see the set of her shoulders. I squeezed her hand and she squeezed back. Whatever happened next, I couldn't have picked a better person to be by my side.

Will and Leith stopped near a small ladder with curved handles, heads close together in conference. Will clapped a hand on Leith's shoulder and nodded before calling to us.

"Turn around, we have to get naked."

"That's no fun," Eve grumbled, but we obliged.

"Count to twenty and then get in the water."

Eve and I both exchanged shocked looks. I turned around to ask if they really were going to murder us but was greeted by two bright white bare asses.

I blinked rapidly, a blush flaring up my neck and into my face as I whipped my head back around.

"You can't peek that's cheating," Eve chided, throwing me a wink.

"Are we going to get in the water?" I asked her. "Like, seriously?"

"You can make yourself a foot tall by thinking about it and you're worried about a night swim?"

"I'm worried about being drowned. Or eaten."

"That second one isn't so bad."

A flash of Leith's mouth on me the night before burned through me and I had to shake my head to clear it. Leith would not hurt me. I knew it, in my very core, like I knew that my luck would work to keep onlookers and rogue joggers away from us.

"Are we at twenty yet?" Eve asked.

"Shit, I thought you were counting."

"You get ditzy when you're horny," Eve teased, then called out over her shoulder, "Ready or not, here we come!"

I gripped Eve's hand like it might keep me from floating away and out into orbit. She placed her free hand on my shoulder, turning me into her.

"C, look at me," she said. "You can't lose your guts now. We're going to jump into the water. Do not stop swimming until you find Leith. On the count of three."

"One..."

"You're something else."

"Two..."

"Could we be something?"

"Two and a half..."

"Eve!"

"What! I'm nervous too!"

I need to risk it.

"Three!" I yelled and took off, pulling off my clothes as I ran until suddenly I was air born and then I hit the frigid water in just my underwear. I resurfaced, gasping for air and willing my body not to freeze from shock.

There was no sign of Leith or Will, just the rapidly darkening waves pushing me around. I paddled in a circle until I realized I was alone. Eve was no longer behind me—I hadn't even heard her jump. Leith and Will had vanished, and I was in the ocean in the dark.

There again was fear, cresting with each wave that rose above me and tightening around my heart. I was just about to turn and swim back to the ladder that sat waiting, rusted and cold, when a dark-haired head appeared in the water in front of me. Leith's grey eyes caught the moon, sparking silver, and as he got closer, I realized something was different about him.

His ears had flattened along the side of his head and his eyes were massive, wide and round like a fish. Gills flared from his neck, delicate like chiffon in the water. He reached out a tentative hand toward me and I could see the speckled pattern of his skin, the webbing stretching between his fingers.

I took his hand, surprised to find the skin smooth and satin-like. He pulled me toward him in the water, catching me securely in his arms and anchoring me against the current. My legs bumped against his bottom half, and I cried out in surprise when I was met instead with a strong, smooth tail ending in a shark-like fin.

The truth left me slack-jawed. I had been so wrong this entire time.

Leith was a merman.

16

Leith

Caoimhe was beautiful in the water, pale limbs stretching through the waves, her blonde hair swirling around her. The curve of her breasts met my chest as we floated together and I imagined, for just a moment, the two of us passionately joined in the water. I had to refocus on the press of the water around us to keep my claspers from sliding free.

"Holy shit," Caoimhe breathed out, eyes wide. "Holy *shit!*" She gripped my biceps and squeezed, kicking happily in the water.

"I can't believe Nan was right! I mean, obviously not the 'dragging me down to the depths and devouring me part.'"

I frowned, hoping it was exaggerated enough to count as playful. With my gills out, I couldn't speak out loud. I couldn't tell her that I would have loved to devour her in the water, but not in any way her grandmother should know about.

"Oh, don't make that face, I know you won't hurt me. Nan is just old school."

I wiggled my eyebrows and nipped at her nose. She shrieked before letting out a low growl and trying to get mine back. She was too short in the water and couldn't get the height she needed.

I smiled wide, feeling the trapped laughter explode in my chest.

"Alright, so, let me get the full effect." Caoimhe pushed off me, treading water. She made a gesture for me to spin. I motioned back for her to give me more space—the full bulk of my tail was obscured in the dark water and I didn't want to accidentally send her flying. But when I obliged, spinning in a tight circle, a tickle of pleasure slid down my spine as she gasped.

"Leith," she said, swimming back up to me again. Her eyes were hooded, her mouth slightly parted. "Would it be rude to...to ask to touch your tail?"

I imagined her small hands sliding along my dorsal, delicately finding where my tail met my spine. A clasper did shoot out and I took a deep breath to get control of myself.

"Oh, I'm sorry. It *is* rude." She shook her head. "Never mind, forget I asked."

I shrugged. Then, I pointed back to the park.

"We're done?" She asked, looking disappointed.

I shook my head so hard I thought it might fly off. I was nowhere near done with her. Especially not now—not now that we had shown our true selves to one another. That kind of freedom didn't just open doors, it kicked them in with a battering ram.

"I'll wait, then," she said, raising her eyebrows. I nodded, then watched as she swam back to the ladder, making sure she wasn't swallowed or stuck beyond the waves.

Once she climbed back up, she turned and waved. Even from here I could see she was shivering. I transformed quickly, hanging from the ladder in the water until I had legs again and then climbed up. It wasn't until I followed Caoimhe's hungry gaze that I remembered I was naked.

Both my cocks twitched in unison, pleased at the attention. I was relieved she wasn't running away screaming but quickly couldn't focus on anything other than the way she was salivating.

"Leith," she said, her voice low.

My cocks twitched again. There was no hiding the effect this woman had on me—not now.

"Are those both for me?" She asked.

"Only for you," I answered, feeling the strain of them against the cold air.

"If I wasn't lucky before, I am now." She cleared the distance between us quickly, running her hands up into my hair and pulling me down to her for a kiss. I pulled her into me, desperate to touch as much of her as I could but her shivering beneath my hands made me pause.

"What's w-w-wrong?" she asked when I pulled away.

"Your lips are blue." I rubbed my hands up and down her arms, working to smooth the goosebumps and get some friction heat into her skin.

"G-g-guess you have to w-w-warm me up."

"At home," I said, laughing when she stuck her tongue out at me.

"You promise?" I lead her back to where our clothes were piled in the grass.

"Absolutely."

"Where are W-w-w-will and Evely-y-yn?"

"Safe, someplace private probably."

She looked worried, pulling her shirt over soaking wet hair as she scanned the dark water.

"Hey," I squeezed her shoulder. "They're safe. I promise."

Caoimhe nodded, but she didn't look like she entirely believed me.

"I can try and go find them, but I don't want the image of what they're doing right now scarred into my brain."

She laughed, still shaking from the cold despite now being fully dressed. "Okay, okay," she said. "I believe you. It's just new for me."

"Me too," I said.

***

Caoimhe had stopped shivering by the time we reached her apartment thanks to both our coats and the brisk walk. A soft flush settled in her cheeks and across her nose. Her curls were crisp, nearly frozen in perfect swirls from being wet in the cold. I thought about crunching them in my palm before wrapping their length around my fingers, pulling back at the base to get a better angle to—

"I think we both need a hot shower," she said, jolting me back to the present. Her apartment was dark and silent, blessedly free of fairy interlopers, friends, or neighbors—for the moment. I nodded, sure my voice would give me away and followed her in.

I was about to settle on the couch and wait for her, but as soon as the door closed, her frigid hands were sliding under my shirt and pulling it over my head. She wiggled out of my coat draped around her shoulders and I helped her with the buttons on her own, pushing it off to the floor and meeting her greedy mouth with mine. We stumbled across the floor, leaving a trail of clothes behind us.

Caoimhe broke free to turn the water on, letting the shower run behind the curtain. She stopped me from stepping in.

"They're old pipes," she said, reaching behind to flip a switch on the wall. "It'll take a second to get warm." Before I had a chance to feel awkward about standing naked in her cold bathroom, she had one of my cocks in her hand, working the shaft and sliding her thumb just beneath the head in a way that sent sparks shooting behind my eyes.

"Do they get jealous of each other?" she asked, tracing her other hand down my stomach to my inner thigh, teasing me.

"Yes, gods yes they do."

"We can't have that," she purred, finally gripping my second cock in an almost identical fashion to the first. I gripped the shower rod for balance, the dual sensation enough to nearly knock me over.

I heard her moving, my eyes closed in pleasure, felt the sudden loss of her heat in front of me only to cry out despite myself as her flat wet tongue licked between both my cocks, pressing against each side simultaneously.

The shower rod gave a dangerous creak but I clung on with one hand, the other reaching down to fist her frozen curls as she slipped the head of the first cock into her mouth, teasing it first with short licks along the shaft. I saw stars again as she licked along the head, but all too soon the sensation was gone, only to be repeated on the second cock.

She was taking her mission for equality very seriously.

Steam began to waft over the top of the curtain and I released her hair, tapping the top of her head lightly. She looked up at me, her mouth still wrapped around one cock and it sent a jolt straight through me.

"In," I managed to choke out and she released me, grinning up from on her knees. She threw me a mock salute and stood.

"Aye, Captain."

The water was perfectly warm, cascading down on us and immediately thawing the ocean's chill. I drank my fill of Caoimhe as she closed her eyes and rinsed her hair out, finally setting her curls free from their frozen hold. She sighed in relief, a softness spreading across her face. I let my eyes wander down the rest of her, taking in the upward sloping shape of her breasts, the soft mound of her stomach, the swirl of dark blonde hair between her legs.

When I looked back up, Caoimhe was staring at me curiously.

I arched my eyebrows and waited.

"You're still human," she said slowly.

"Yes."

She gestured around us and pointed up at the showerhead.

"Hello, you're wet?"

"So are you, I hope," I growled, stepping closer.

"But mermaids change in water," she said, ignoring my advance.

"Can I tell you all our secrets later?"

"No more secrets," she gave me a playful shove. "I've had enough to last me multiple lifetimes."

"We don't change in all water," I said, giving in. "It's an adaptation for living with humans. If we changed every time it rained, we'd never make it as a species.

"And," I continued, reaching to cup her perfect ass in my hands. "It lets us have shower sex with leprechaun women."

She laughed, pressing into me and I felt her body flex to get closer. "That's a very specific evolutionary advantage."

Before she could ask any other questions, I angled my mouth over hers, my tongue exploring her mouth.

I reached between us, feeling my cocks grow even harder at the warm slick between her legs. I found her clit and worked it in small circles, gaining speed as she moaned into my mouth. I was growing desperate, the tightness nearly unbearable in my cock and balls. I needed to be inside her, but I also didn't want to rush.

Caoimhe gripped my wrist and whispered, "Wait," against my mouth. I stopped immediately, pulling away just enough to check her face. Her lips were plumped from kissing, her eyes hazy and bright with need.

"I want your cocks," she said. Then licked her lips, glancing down and back up at me. "Now," she added.

17

Caoimhe

Leith met my demand immediately, lifting me up and bracing me against the shower wall. I wrapped my legs around him and clung on tight, lifting my hips to give him the best access to my pussy.

The first cock slid in easily, delicious pressure against my needy walls and I sighed at the sensation I'd been desperate for. Leith set the head of his second cock at my entrance but hesitated.

"Are you sure?" He asked, breathless in his restraint.

I nodded, shifting against him for friction, going crazy at the sudden pause. I was more sure in that moment than I had ever been. I wanted all of him. I would take whatever he would give, no matter how much or how little.

"Tell me if it gets uncomfortable," he said.

"I have something to show you still," I said, need making my voice crack. "You have to trust me."

"I do," he said, and slid the second cock in alongside the second. I felt myself expand to accommodate his double girth and we moaned in unison at the connection.

He began thrusting, slowly at first, letting both of us adjust for a few moments before picking up the pace. It was a perfect fit, his double cocks inside my greedy pussy, expanding before clenching around him, sending white heat through my vision as I clung on. I'd never been filled like this before. All those years of disappointment vanished, leaving only the friction of Leith inside me.

I angled my hips to better rub my clit along his length but Leith held me in place against the wall. He reached down between us, pulling back slowly until his cocks were nearly free. I glanced down at the slick lengths of him and watched as they slid in and out of me, letting my mind slip into the frenzied heat between us.

"Ready?" he breathed in my ear and I nodded.

He picked up speed, slamming into me harder and harder as he went, the pressure in my core growing to a white hot point that we were both chasing. Just as I was sure I would come, he reached down and pinched my clit, sending me over the screaming edge. I was a hazy, floating mess, lost in the stratosphere. Somewhere far away I heard Leith finish, felt him sag against me. I barely registered that the water was cold now.

Gently, Leith slid out of me and helped me to stand on my own, steadying me against him. My legs were jello and my knees threatened to give up. He reached around me and turned the water off, pushing the curtain back.

"Oh, warm towels," I groaned. "I am the smartest woman alive."

I carefully stepped from the shower, grabbing one of the towels from the warming rack I turned on earlier. It was like stepping into the sun on a clear day, except it was in my hands and also incredibly fluffy. I handed Leith the other and felt my heart backflip at the joyous surprise on his face.

"How did you do that?" he asked, rubbing the towel gleefully all over his face and chest before wrapping it around his waist.

"Magic," I said, wiggling my fingers through the air.

"I didn't know leprechauns were renowned for warming towels."

I led the way from the bathroom and into the bedroom, rooting through my dresser to see if I had anything that might fit him.

"I also didn't know you could…accommodate so much," he said, voice growing rough again. The sound hit my pussy directly and I felt an ache. There was *no way* I was ready to go again already. Did he also have magic dicks?

I grinned, feeling heat tickle back up my spine at the very thought of all of him pressed inside me. "Call it our own adaptation," I said. His eyes darkened and he gave me that addictive half-smile.

"Nature seems to have made us for each other," he said. He meant it as a joke but something about the delivery felt too real.

Maybe, said that voice again. *Just maybe.*

"You're going to have to sleep naked," I said.

He put a hand against his chest and feigned annoyance.

"Oh no," he said. "What will I do?" He nearly flung the towel across the room as he crawled into my bed. I couldn't help looking hungrily at both of his dicks swinging before hitting the blankets.

The sound of my front door opening was accompanied by Eve's voice as she shouted out, "You are never going to guess what I just did."

"I think you can," Leith said, resting his head on his arm. I had to physically stop myself from crawling over to lick his bicep.

"Don't move," I pointed to him threateningly as I slipped into my robe. I stepped out to meet Eve, closing the bedroom door behind me.

"Oh," Eve said cocking her head to the side as she slid out of her jacket. "Ohhhhhh." She grinned salaciously and stuck her tongue out between her teeth, breaking into a hip-wiggling dance. "You know *exactly* what I just did."

I laughed and swatted at her, trying to get her attention. She continued dancing, singing some pop song with filthy lyrics. When she finally stopped, she clasped her hands together dramatically and leaned into me.

"Was it good?"

I pointed emphatically to the bedroom door and whispered, "Not now."

Eve's grin spread wider and she clapped her hands together as if starting official business. "That's perfect, I'll get Will to bring spare PJs before he comes over."

"Comes over?"

"Yeah, someone has to stop the four of us from fucking each other into a UTI and I know just the man."

"Eve no," I groaned, my shoulders sagging.

"My man Bobby!" She flung an all-important arm into the air, pointing a single finger to the sky. "Crushing the male libido since 2008. Besides, Will's never seen *My Light, My Blood.* Can you even believe?"

She was gone again before I could protest, swinging the door shut behind her in yet another flurry of pop lyrics. I heard my bedroom door creak open and Leith's voice came from the other side.

"What's *My Light, My Blood?*"

***

"My god," Leith whispered, a fistful of popcorn stuck in the air in front of his mouth. "He's beautiful."

The four of us were piled onto my couch beneath all the blankets we had between both apartments. Bobby Robertson was sparkling for the first time on screen and Leith's face was reverent.

"See!" Eve said around a mouthful of popcorn, kicking her feet out from under the blankets. "He gets it."

"You don't think he's beautiful?" Leith looked down at me. I was comfortably under his arm, resting my head on his shoulder. We were both finally dry and Leith was wearing some of Will's old sweatpants and flannel. He smelled lightly of cigarettes but it wasn't off-putting. He was still warm and soft, entirely himself within the folds of the blankets.

I shook my head. "I think he looks like he was rude to the makeup team," I said.

"Is that what's so off?" Will asked, a ginger ale resting on his knee, his other hand holding the popcorn bucket for Eve.

"Hater," Eve shot back.

It felt as if we'd been doing this for years, the four us tucked in together watching a movie as the wind began to pick up outside. I tucked my feet up onto the couch, burrowing further into the blankets and snuggling into Leith.

Maybe he was right. Maybe we had been made just for each other.

I listened to Eve begin her rant about what she claimed were societal-level slights against the lead actors of the movie, drifting to sleep in the comfort of Leith's arms.

When I woke up, I was slightly disoriented, realizing it was now pitch black and I was not on the couch. Warm arms were wrapped around me and I could feel Leith's breath on the back of my neck. I started to turn over but he clamped down around me.

"No," he murmured, half awake.

"I have to pee," I said, wiggling against him. There was a sharp inhale and he moved an arm down to my hip, holding it in place.

"Don't," he said, burrowing into my neck.

"Don't what?" I asked, wiggling again. I was surprised to feel stiffness pushing against my thigh. It had to be like three a.m.

"You know," he growled.

"If you set me free, I promise to behave," I said.

"You won't," but he lifted his arms so I could tip-toe to the bathroom.

The bathroom light was harsh after so much darkness and I was startled at how wild my hair had dried, pillowing out around me in frizzy waves. There was a dark bruise developing on my neck the exact size of Leith's mouth. I washed my hands, brushed my teeth, and tried to think sleepy thoughts.

But all I could think about were Leith's cocks.

I stepped quietly back into the bedroom where I could see Leith's chest rising and falling at a slow and even pace. Sliding under the covers, I rolled into the hollow of his back, throwing my arm over his waist and inhaling the musky, briny smell of him.

I wondered for a moment how I'd gotten here, half-awake, horny as hell, pressed into a practical stranger—a stranger who I'd entrusted my entire life to in less than a week.

Was it really nature at work or was something else leading us to one another?

Leith's calloused hands closed over mine.

"Awake?" he murmured and I nodded into his back.

"Good," he said, voice rough with sleep and something else. He rolled over, bracing himself on either side of me and kissed me softly. I could feel his twin cocks stiffening beneath his sweatpants and I lifted my hips to meet him. Nothing felt as good as being filled with Leith and I was ready for more, growing wet with the very memory of riding him.

I reached down between us, sliding my hands into his sweats and finding the silky skin of his cock there. I gripped one and then the other, unable to work my other hand in to help. But Leith quickly grabbed my hand and laced our fingers together, pressing it to the bed by my head.

He let go to move to my shirt, exposing my aching nipples. He dipped his head down and nipped at each before I couldn't take it anymore.

"You have to fuck me," I pleaded, breathless with want.

"Have to?" He asked before licking rapidly across the very tip of my nipple. I arched into him, digging my fingers into his back.

"Please, Leith," I said. "Please, fuck me."

He groaned into my neck, fumbling with the edge of his sweats. I wriggled to shove my own pajama bottoms down and we met back together in an awkward half-dressed tangle.

I didn't care. I spread my legs and shifted my hips to give him better access, reaching down to guide the first cock to my entrance. It slid in easily, and I lifted my hips against him, desperately shifting for more friction, more pressure, more of him. The second cock slid in against the first one and a moan escaped my lips at the full sensation.

Leith slid a hand behind my lower back and pressed up, rolling us both over so that I was on top of him but we stayed connected.

"I want to see you," he said. I didn't need further encouragement, immediately spurred on by the new angle of his cocks inside me. They hit the walls of my pussy at that precious sweet spot that made me see stars and I was able to better grind my clit against one of his shafts. I sat up straighter, riding faster and faster as Leith gripped my hips, urging me on. I could feel my tits bouncing loose in the air from the effort as sweat slid down my spine.

Leith sat forward and the fresh angle pressed his cocks against both the front and back wall of my pussy simultaneously, applying new friction to my clit. I cried out, coming in a blinding flash, feeling the clench of my cunt around his double girth.

We gently untangled ourselves from one another so that I was resting on his chest, one arm wrapped around my shoulders. I watched the heaving rise and fall of his chest as we both caught our breath.

"I might get addicted to that," I said.

"You can have it whenever you want," he said.

"But when will we sleep?"

"When we're dead." He kissed my forehead and a few moments later I heard the tell-tale soft snore of deep sleep. I drifted off again to the sound of the garbage trucks trundling down the road and the earliest birds beginning to wake.

18

Leith

I woke up to my phone ringing.

"Rise and shine, Romeo," Kelly snapped through the line.

I pulled the phone away to check the time. It was barely nine.

"No games, Kel," I said, sleep still gripping me. Caoimhe stirred next to me, flopping an arm over my waist. I wasn't getting up any sooner than I had to and Mister Flipper didn't open until noon.

"All the games, Leith honey, literally."

"Shit," I bolted up. I had entirely forgotten, in all the chaos of the last two days, that we were setting up for the carnival that morning.

"Yeah, I thought so."

"I'll be right there," I was about to hang up but Kelly stopped me.

"Bring Caoimhe," she said.

I froze. Did she know?

"I know," she said. "Will beat you here."

I wasn't sure what her reaction would be to our latest developments with Caoimhe and Evelyn. Caoimhe at least wasn't human, but Eve could be a risk. Kelly would be livid we'd risked our safety—and hers by association—for what she would assume was a fling.

I looked back at Caoimhe, sprawled across the bed, her shirt hitched up around her waist revealing a creamy swath of skin. A drool spot was pooling under her on the pillow and her face was slack in sleep.

Between waking her up and sneaking out, I decided it was better to at least say good morning before I left. Careful not to lay back down in case I never got back up, I leaned over, inhaling the smell of her before kissing her once on the temple. She stirred but didn't open her eyes.

"Hey," I tried, running a hand across her curls. "Caoimhe." She rolled into my hand, nuzzling against it and I felt my heart swell.

"I have to go," I said. At that, her eyes popped open and her softened face immediately folded into a frown. "It's carnival setup."

Her eyes widened and she snorted in a sharp inhale, sitting up.

"Shit, I said I'd help."

"When?"

She shot me a look and leapt out of bed, rifling through her closet.

"When I was off being good at my job." Her voice was muffled from where she'd poked it between various layers off coats and dresses. I slid into my jeans and shirt from the day before, all too aware what Kelly would have to say about it when I showed up. If she knew, she knew—might as well not make myself later than I had to just for a different t-shirt.

"I guess I'll see you there." Why was I suddenly nervous? The light of day made all of the intimate revelations from the last night feel unreal. It was as if I'd dreamed them and awoke to find only some parts were actually happening.

Caoimhe's smiling face emerged from within the closet. She had several pairs of pants draped over one arm and a blouse dangling from the other.

"Absolutely," she said, echoing my promise from the beach last night. Warmth spread through my chest and into the rest of me, buoyant and thrilling. "I'd go with you but I have some other work to do this morning first. I'll meet you there in about an hour or so."

I nodded, feeling a smile break free from my worries, and gathered up my things.

I had a hand on the door when Caoimhe's voice stopped me.

"Excuse me?" She called from the bedroom and I froze. "That's it?"

"What?"

She appeared in the hall, half-dressed, her hair clipped up away from her face.

"Sure, alright, show the girl you're a merman, blow her mind in bed, and then just bounce without a goodbye kiss." She waggled her hands in the air sarcastically. "Keep it real casual I see how it is."

I cleared the distance between us before I realized what I was doing and kissed her. I let myself sink into the kiss like I had so often sunk into the water, letting go of everything else to simply exist in the soothing abyss. When I resurfaced, Caoimhe's eyes were still closed, her mouth still half-open.

"Better?" I asked, stomping down the urge to fill her mouth with other things when it looked so inviting.

She opened her eyes, hooded with the same lust I felt pooling in me, and nodded.

"You better go," she said, voice low.

"Or?"

"Or we'll never leave this apartment again."

I smiled, letting fresh, new warmth explode through me as I stepped away from her.

"You say that like it's a bad thing."

"Some of us have to work."

"Do we?"

"Bye, Leith," she said, swatting my hands away and stepping back into her bedroom, a shy smile peeking out from under her curls.

"Bye, Caoimhe."

Outside the air was crisp and wet, full of the promise that comes after a morning's rain. I decided to stop in for a coffee on the way, knowing it would help to smooth over Kelly's mood. She didn't usually care for it, but I knew she had a soft-spot for a unique seasonal drink—not pumpkin spice, but something in that vein. One of the cafes along the harbor had an apple crisp latte with cinnamon crunch candies sprinkled across the top and if that didn't get me out of trouble with the Mister Flipper's manager then nothing would.

I wasn't paying attention as I swung the door open because I slammed smack into a middle-aged woman with piles of blonde curls twisted up on her head. Her coffee went flying and we both yelled in surprise.

I frantically apologized and dipped down to grab the cup from the floor before looking up and locking eyes with the spitting image of Caoimhe in twenty years. I froze.

"It's okay," she said. "We all get into a rush some days." But it clearly was not okay. She was scowling at me tightly as she shook the coffee off her hands and arms.

"I'm late for work," I managed to get out. How was someone so identical to Caoimhe standing in front of me? I realized then with a flush of shame that I knew nothing about her family—I had automatically assumed as a magical creature living among humans that she was entirely alone like me. Of course she wasn't.

"Must be a doctor or something else incredibly *urgent*," she said.

"I'm a tour boat operator," I said, embarrassment growing by the second. "Let me replace your coffee, I'm so sorry."

Something crept across her face—curiosity or suspicion—but she nodded.

A small line made it so that we had to stand in silence and I wasn't sure how to cut the awkward tension between us. The woman stepped away for a moment to grab a fistful of napkins from the station stacked with creamer and sugar before returning.

"What tour company do you work for?" she finally offered, dabbing at her clothes with the napkins.

"Mister Flipper," I said and watched that strange look on her face a second time.

"You know Caoimhe Ryan, then."

I felt myself rooted to the spot, the entire world zeroing in on what the woman had just said. Was this a trap?

"I thought so," she said, and I realized my face must've given me away. "I'm her mother."

Well that explained the likeness. We stepped up to the counter where I ordered in a haze. I didn't even hear what Mrs. Ryan ordered. I paid, then we stepped to the side to wait. I prayed to whatever gods were listening that she had gotten just a black coffee and would soon be on her way, but no one seemed to be listening.

"It's dangerous here for her," she said, leaning into me. She smelled earthy but sharp, as if she had turned the dirt in her garden into a perfume. "I don't have to tell someone like you that. You know."

I knew all too well.

"She could be safe," her mother continued. "With me and her grandmother back in our lands. We're powerful there. The humans can't hurt us."

"What are you saying?" Our coffees slid across the counter and the barista's smile wavered, sensing the tension sparking off of us.

"Just that, for someone with your *abilities…*" she paused and looked me up and down. I felt exposed. "Would Ireland be so far to swim if it meant someone they cared for was safe?"

"How did you—"

She cut me off with a sharp nod toward the door of the cafe. I noticed then a green-skinned fairy perched above the door jamb. As the door swung open and a new customer entered, the fairy let loose a chime-like giggle—the sound of a bell alerting the barista to a new guest.

"I did not leave my daughter entirely exposed," Mrs. Ryan said.

"There is not much that has escaped my ears over the few years I've been gone. You are both lucky I'm not so unforgiving as her grandmother."

"Does Caoimhe want to leave?" I suddenly found myself torn between wanting to see her every day and her continued safety. I hated myself for not immediately choosing what was better for her and not for me.

But what I wanted didn't matter.

"No," her mother said, pursing her lips. "But she might listen to an outside influence."

I nodded.

"I'm sorry, again, for the coffee. It was nice to meet you." I started to walk away but her voice caught me before I could leave.

"You would be welcome with us, you know."

I nodded, stepping back out into the sunlight, all the warmth and promise of the morning deflated in my gut.

19

Caoimhe

Kelly gave me an icy nod as I walked up to where she and Will directed a massive delivery truck to unload along the dock.

"Caoimhe!" Will waved with one hand, pointing to the delivery men with the other. "We got games!"

"You always had game," I quipped back. He laughed as the two men passed by him, each holding an end of a massive dart board peppered with holes.

"We got balloon darts, ring toss, and bottle smash. All the classics."

I glanced over at Kelly who made eye contact before turning on her heel and walking into her office, slamming the door behind her. It echoed off the nearby boats and I couldn't help but wince.

"Ignore her," Will said. "She's mad at me."

"Really? 'Cause it looks like she's mad at me."

"Sirens who can't scream get pent up in all sorts of ways, let her work it off."

"A siren?" I gasped. I'd only ever heard of them. Nothing about Kelly had been a giveaway to her true nature. But then, neither had anything about Will and Leith. Except...

"Hey, did you guys hate the dunk-tank idea because—"

"Yup," Will cut me off as the delivery men walked by us back into the truck. "That's exactly why."

Because to be submerged in water meant revealing their true forms to a bunch of humans they were trying to win back over.

I wondered for a split second if Leith's internet notoriety would be positively or negatively impacted if people knew the truth. Mom said there was magic everywhere, but we had to be willing to risk it.

I'd risked everything with Leith and the result had me practically floating around with happiness. I wanted everyone to know him the way I did. I wanted a world where we both could be our entire true selves freely, safely.

My morning optimism believed maybe someday that world could be in Boston.

As if on cue, Will hollered and I turned to see Leith walking down the pier to us. He had a coffee cup clutched in one hand, the other shoved in his jacket. His shoulders were hunched and the former stormy scowl I knew from our first meeting was firmly back in place. I wondered where he'd been—I assumed he'd beat me to the pier.

"We have to talk," he said when he reached me, not even slowing his steps. All my buoyancy deflated. "Stay right there." He continued walking past me and into the office, letting the door shut only slightly more gently than Kelly had.

"Now *he's* mad at you," Will said, smiling mockingly. I resisted the urge to smack it off his face.

"I'm gonna tell Eve you hit on me the first day we met," I said in a deadpan.

"Don't!" He whined, immediately whirling around. "She'll be so mad. Forget what I said, Leith's just in a mood like Kelly."

I threw him a look and picked up the nearest box of carnival supplies—it looked like tablecloths and flags—hauling them away toward where the delivery guys had started to assemble the booths.

A few hours later, everyone intensely focused on the task at hand and on avoiding one another, we had a fully assembled carnival. Incredible what four adults with unresolved tension between them could accomplish when they set their mind to it.

I offered to go and pick up lunch for us while Leith and Will took out the first tour of the day. I winced as young voices chanted, "Dunk man!" from near the boat. Thankfully, they only had two tours for the day. Kelly announced they'd be closing early to kick off the carnival, and we drafted up a quick email to send to the last tour of the day inviting them to be the first prizewinners for the night.

It was going to be me and Kelly when I got back, so I took my time, wandering up the street and peeking in small restaurants along the way. Kelly hadn't intimidated me until I discovered she could drive someone insane by opening her mouth—if she wanted. I wasn't eager to find out if I was on her shit list.

And something else was nagging at me. Something about the way Leith's entire demeanor had suddenly shifted in the course of an hour. We went from dizzy over one another to not even saying a full sentence.

Doubt crept in, worrying its fingers across my sleep-deprived mind. Maybe he'd changed his mind. Maybe he wasn't who I'd thought.

Maybe I made a huge mistake and all of this had been for nothing.

I tried to resuscitate the wild hope I had that morning—that there was more in the world worth trusting than I'd been taught. That people could be good and kind and worthy. But there was no bringing it back to life. I felt myself quickly sinking into old beliefs and by the time I ordered several trays of spicy noodles and egg rolls to carry back to the office, I boxed up my feelings for Leith and packed them in the farthest closet I had in my heart.

I was good at publicity but I was exceptional at disappointment. Leith would be just another man who let me down.

I'd tell him we didn't have to do the whole song and dance when he got back. He could be free of me and I'd go on my way after the carnival.

The world tilted at the thought and I suddenly couldn't breathe. I thought of his eyes, soft on me that morning, his calloused hand against my cheek as he kissed me. I thought of the wildly beautiful shape of him in the water, strong and sure against the current even as I tried desperately to stay afloat.

I couldn't do this.

Maybe there was no world for us out there. Not in Boston, not anywhere.

I thought of Mom and my grandmother, calling me to Ireland with them. I wiped away the beginning of hot tears in my eyes and tried again to box up Leith, to break free of his grip on my heart by imagining a new life in a new country, away from Boston and all its memories.

Maybe what I truly needed was a fresh start. Someplace where I could be true to myself and stop hiding.

I thought I'd found it here, squashed on the couch between friends.

I packed up that memory too.

Striding across the pier, I pushed my shoulders back, found my best professional smile, and knocked on the office door.

"No," came Kelly's voice from within.

"Lunch!" I called back.

"Fine." I heard her footsteps and then a loud, popping click of metal on metal before the door swung open. "Dirty trick to use food."

"Will said you were only mad at him," I said, handing her a plastic tray filled to the brim with hot, spicy, perfect carbs.

"No, you're on my shit list too," she said. "But I don't like to rip new assholes before lunch." She jerked her head inside and I followed her, settling uneasily into one of the metal chairs across the desk.

"If there's anything I can improve upon as your publicist, I'd—"

"Stop bringing humans around," she snapped, popping open the container and cramming a large forkful of noodles into her mouth with a vengeance.

"Kelly, respectfully, you bring literal boatfuls of humans around multiple times a day."

"They're not fucking Will."

Was she jealous? Or was it something else?

"I hope not, that'd be a lot of work for just him." I thought a joke might help lighten the mood. I was wrong.

Kelly glared at me, setting her fork down. "You don't get it," she said. "We lost one of our own, not too long ago. It's different for us. Simply existing is enough to get us captured, tortured, and killed. And you come wiggling in here with your human friend—"

"I do *not* wiggle."

"—exposing yourself and then Leith and Will—"

"I didn't expose them! They—"

"—which puts all the rest of us in danger! You have no idea what you've done, what you're risking, by trusting that human."

I wasn't hungry anymore. This entire effort had been a mistake.

"I trust Evelyn with my life. More so now that she knows the truth," I said. "And you can ask Will—he made that choice for himself and he'll tell you the same."

I stood, taking the other containers of noodles with me. "You don't have to worry about me 'wiggling' around for much longer anyway." I spit the words out like they were too venomous to keep in my mouth before storming out of the office just in time to slam into Leith. The noodle boxes crunched between us, sending lunch flying across the dock and smearing the spicy red sauce across us both.

"That's two for two," Leith muttered.

"What the fuck are you talking about?" I threw my hands in the air. "Whatever! Now that you're here, I can rip this band-aid off too."

"What are *you* talking about?" His brows furrowed and his mouth pulled down in that infuriating way that made me want to kiss him.

"You don't have to dump me," I said, all too aware that the guests disembarking could hear my every word. "I'll save you the trouble and tell you I'm good. We're good. I'll be out of your stupid pirate hair after the carnival."

His hair was not stupid, and it was only a little bit piratey, shaggy and windswept along his shoulders. The stupid, handsome fucker.

Leith glanced sidelong around us, before gripping my arm and hauling me back into the office.

"Can I get some privacy?" Kelly's voice was shrill around a mouthful of noodles.

"It'll just be a second," Leith said then turned to me, his hand still on my arm. "Who said I wanted to dump you?"

"You so much as did when you came stomping by all 'we need to talk! I'm not going to stop to finish the sentence because I'm walking so fast! Mmrrr HARUMPH!'" I threw my arms around again for emphasis. I was being absolutely ridiculous but I was past the point of caring. This shit needed to be put in the heart closet faster than it was happening. I could feel tears building again, hot behind my eyes.

I would not cry in front of Kelly.

"Is it dumping if you've only been together three days?" The offending party intoned, pretending to sound bored.

"One second," Leith snapped at Kelly without turning his head, keeping his gaze fixed on me. "Your mom said you could go somewhere safe, away from humans, where you'd be powerful. But you said no. Why?"

It wasn't a question. It was a demand. One that I decided to ignore.

"My mom?" I sputtered. "My fucking mom?"

"I bumped into her today—"

I barked out a laugh, cutting him off. "Of all the fucking luck in the world, of course she uses hers to sniff you out."

"What are you talking about?"

"I already told her I wouldn't leave Boston," I said, a cold fury building in my chest. So I couldn't trust humans, I thought to myself, mentally checking off a list. I couldn't trust mermen, and now, apparently, I couldn't trust my own mom. "All she had to do was use her little fairy spies, think about running into you, and then wait around for it to happen."

"That's it?" Kelly said.

"Hum 'Twinkle Twinkle,' right now, I dare you," I snapped. "See how complicated your powers actually are."

"Girl, you *wish*—"

"Stop, both of you." Leith's voice boomed out over the top of us and despite myself I felt my pussy clench. This was *not* the time. But he was standing straight, heat building in his gaze as he stared at me, and the commanding thing was apparently really doing it for me in that moment.

Because everything feels out of control.

"Kel, please let us use the office," he said, finally breaking away from my face to glance to where the manager was glaring daggers at me.

"No," she said.

"Kel, please," he said. "For just a—"

"A fucking second, yes, you've said. Gods above and below, *fine.*" She closed the box of noodles and grabbed her phone. She pushed past us in a huff but paused in the doorway, leveling a finger at Leith. "If you fuck in here, I will know, and there will be more than hell to pay."

"No chance of that happening," I muttered and Kelly rolled her eyes before slamming the office door behind her. I wondered how much more of her temper the poor hinges could take.

"She offered to let me go with you," he said.

"Kelly?" I squinted at him, confused.

"Your mom," he said. "She said I'd be welcome with you both, if you left."

"Well I'm not leaving, so go off to Ireland yourself then."

"Caoimhe," he said, and I hated how much I loved hearing him say my name like that—low and soft, like he was saying something more. "I won't be able to live with myself if something happens to you. Not when I know you could've been safe."

"I've lived in Boston my entire life," I said, unable to look anywhere but his stormy gray eyes. "And no one has ever found me out."

I didn't entirely believe what I was saying. Police lights flashed across my mind, and tears began to slide down my cheeks as I remembered my dad's kind face and crooked grin. There was a reason we were all so afraid.

But something in my heart wouldn't let the fear win out. It kept whispering to me, *maybe*, over and over again.

There had to be a way for us to build safety—together.

Leith rubbed his thumb across the tears tracking down my face and I could've lived inside that calloused touch.

"Then why is your mom so terrified?" he asked. He led me to one of the office chairs and I sat with a thud while he perched on the edge of Kelly's desk, never letting go of my hand.

"A human killed my dad," I said, realizing I never had space to say it out loud before. Who could I have confessed to? Until yesterday, not even Eve had known the truth. The overwhelm of it hit me, threatening to drown me in paralyzing sorrow.

I leaned my head into my hands and let the tears come fully, sobbing into my palms. I felt so lost, and so lonely, right when I thought I found people I could call mine. I was tired of hiding, but even more tired of being afraid and I just wanted to feel comfortable in the only place I'd ever known as home. The brief taste I had these last few days was threatening to pull out from under me, whether or not I pushed Leith away, and I couldn't stand it.

"Oh, Caoimhe," he said, kneeling on the office floor and gently wrapping his arms around me. I let him, tipping my head to land on his shoulder while I continued to sob, letting out the grief and fear I'd been holding for years.

After a few minutes, I was able to take a deep breath and I pulled away, wiping my face and snot on my shirt sleeves. I left a sizeable wet patch on Leith's shoulder. He offered me his sleeve as well and I shamelessly took it.

"Real sexy," I said looking down at the streak of snot I left on his sleeve.

"Hey," he said, tilting my face back to his. "I'd rather have all of you, snot and all, than only a few pieces."

I tried to return his half-smile but tears were threatening to build up again.

"We have to give Kelly her office back," I said between sniffles.

"Probably," he said, standing. He offered me his hands and I took them, standing to meet him. "But I have a better idea."

20

Leith

The bottles smashed with a clatter to the ground. Caoimhe threw her arms in the air with a triumph yell.

"You're right, this *does* feel good!" She wound her arm back and launched a second ball at another stack of bottles. The poor plastic bastards never stood a chance.

"You're headed for the Majors next!" I teased. It was a relief to see her laughing and happy again after watching her entirely unravel in Kelly's office. I had no idea something so horrible happened to Caoimhe's family, but now the way she dodged answers on our first date made more sense. She'd been holding on to so much by herself and none of us had any idea.

A murmuring wave of chatter slid toward us from the pier. Will must've returned with the last tour for the day. I would apologize for leaving him solo later.

"Here comes your adoring public," Caoimhe sighed, setting down the third ball. "Come on." She took my hand and led me around the back of the booth.

We were protected from sight by the temporary games, with the water stretching out behind us. The boats that were usually next door must've taken off for the weekend, leaving large empty swathes of water lapping at the structural poles. I could see a stretch of empty dirt and debris, dirty but dry, down below. I'd never noticed it before and I made a note for my next swim in case Kelly was using the office.

"I can't hide here all night," I protested.

"No," she said. "No more hiding." She pulled me to her for a kiss, simple but deep and I had the brief hope that she'd always kiss me like that. *Put that one away for now.*

"Thank you," she said, pulling away. "For earlier. I'm sorry I freaked, it's just…"

"A lot," I offered.

She nodded, offering me a half smile and tugged on the end of my hair playfully. "And I'm sorry I said your hair was piratey."

"Wait, when did you say that?"

"You've got the balloon darts next door, I call dibs on the bottles!" She danced away from me and leapt into the booth just as the guests began to mill around the games and the toasted nuts stand that was wafting tempting smells into the air.

I took up my post at the balloon darts game, trying not to feel too on-display within the thin wood walls around me. This whole thing began to feel like a bad idea. How did Caoimhe know no one was going to descend on me like seals on a school of sardines?

A mom and two boys came up first. They each had one of her hands and they pulled her straight up to the counter that separated us. One of them, wearing a backwards baseball cap and a smear of chocolate on his cheek, pointed up at the stuffed red bear hanging from the edge of the booth.

"That one! That one!"

"You have to win it, sweetheart," she said, looking to me for help.

I nodded, then pointed to the bear. "You can only win that bear if you pop three balloons." I tossed a dart and the balloon popped with a satisfying sound.

The boys' eyes grew wide with glee. The second boy, wearing wraparound pop-bottle glasses, tugged on his mom's hand.

"We can do it! We can win it!"

"How much?" she asked, releasing her hold on the second boy to rummage through her purse.

"It's on us tonight, ma'am," I explained. "It's to better connect with our community members."

"Oh, that's sweet," she said, distracted as the first boy with the ballcap started leaping up and down with her arm as a bungee cord.

"Here buddy," I leaned down to get Ballcap's attention, handing him three darts with the fan-end first, warning him to be careful.

He let fly all three darts, managing to finally pop a balloon on his third try. We all cheered but the moment was quickly overshadowed when I heard an all-too-familiar call from a few teenagers walking directly behind the mom.

"Dunk man! No way!" By now, I realized, the pier had begun to fill and a not-so-small crowd was milling between the games. Several heads whipped around as the herd of teens pressed into the booth, nearly taking out the mom and her kid. They shouted, lifting their phones and competing for my attention, trying to get me to look in turn at each camera. I felt helpless, boxed in—trapped.

A sudden whistle of air and one of the kids dropped their phone, yelling as it slid through the cracks in the boards and hit the water with a muted splash.

"Whoops!" Caoimhe called from the next booth. "My bad! You guys should really go somewhere else before another foul ball knocks down the rest of your phones."

"That's not fair!" One called from somewhere in the middle of the pack.

Another whistle of air, another muted splash.

"I warned you!"

The kids scattered likes rats caught in the sun. I turned to see Caoimhe throw me a wink.

I was in love.

A woman's scream cut the air, freezing everyone on the spot.

"Help! My son! Forest! My son is in the water!"

Without thinking, I leapt over the counter toward the sound of the woman, finding the mom and her son from before standing behind the booths facing the water—where Caoimhe and I had shared a kiss only moments before. She was clutching on to Ballcap, both of them were sobbing, and pointing down into the water below. Sure enough, the little boy with the pop-bottle glasses kept popping up and down through the waves.

Not good.

It would take too long for anyone to get down to that secluded patch of dirt. Shit, I'd been working this job for years and I still didn't know how to get down there. The kid could drown by then, never mind the frigid water and the current.

I slid out of my coat, letting instinct guide my actions, and dove down into the water.

The waves were like a slap to the chest and I was disoriented for a moment under the surface. I had to roll myself, looking for light above and pushing toward it, finally breaking back up above the water.

I had to act fast, I could already feel the change taking hold, could already feel the long snap of my spine stretching into my dorsal fin and the tell-tale fusion of my feet into my tail. Sputtered tiny gasps came from directly to my right and I spotted the kid, flailing his arms in the water. I kicked once, hard, and scooped him easily, holding him above the water as he choked out water.

Hold on, kid, I thought as I felt my gills sprout along my neck. I ducked further into the water to try and hide them, all too aware that I had an audience.

"Holy shit there's a shark in the water with them!"

The mom screamed again, higher and more frightened this time.

Of course they couldn't see that the fins were mine from that high up. All they'd see was me swimming with the kid and what looked like a shark directly on top of us.

This was getting worse the longer it went on.

We were only a few feet from the beach and the water was getting dangerously shallow. I looked over to Glasses, hoping to let him doggy paddle the rest of the way and avoid entirely revealing myself to a literal carnival full of people.

His little face was pale, his lips turning blue, and his eyes were closed.

Shit, shit, double shitting hell.

There was nothing else to be done.

I pushed myself up into the shallows, crawling until we hit the trash-covered beach and I could set the kid down. Screams and shouts erupted from the pier above me, like the soundtrack from a '50s horror movie. I tried to tune them out.

I placed a webbed hand over the kid's chest. My instincts told me he wasn't dead and the muted thumping beneath my palm confirmed it. I tried to run myself through the first aid training we had to renew every year.

Steady compressions, but not with both fists like for an adult. Breathe into both the mouth and the nose, but for a shorter amount of time.

If I got this wrong and killed this kid, I was doomed. I'd be shot on the spot.

Death didn't seem so bad compared to the alternative—a life of exile, away from Will, Kelly, and Caoimhe.

I rolled the kid to his side and gave him a firm thump on the back. He coughed almost immediately, spewing seawater up onto the beach and immediately letting loose a loud wail. Well good, his lungs still worked.

I motioned for him to stay, which was a mistake because he took one look at me and started crying harder, scrambling away from me and up the beach.

"Hey!" A man's voice cried out from somewhere nearby—definitely not from above. "Stay where you are and put both hands where I can see them!"

Not today, buddy.

I turned and vaulted back into the water, using every ounce of strength I had to clear the sand and hit the waves. I kicked my tail, powering away, and I didn't stop until I was sure I was clear of the pier.

Only then did I turn around to check if I was being followed. No one was behind me, the attention of the pier turned almost entirely on the scene on the beach.

No one, except for one lone figure at the end of the pier, staring out after me as the sun flashed in her golden curls.

21

Caoimhe

It had been days since I last saw Leith, swimming out into the harbor after rescuing that kid. Will promised me he was just laying low, trying to stay safe while Boston was in uproar over the new "Harbor Monster" that had been sighted.

But it didn't stop me from leaping for my phone every time it started to ring.

Unfortunately, that meant my grandmother yelled at me more in the last four days than she had in my entire life simply by opportunity.

So when the call lit up my screen again, I knew better. I hit the ignore button and went back to staring at *Kissing Strange Men to Get Married*. I started the show from the beginning, giving me twenty years' worth of episodes to slog through while pretending I didn't exist.

I was doing a pretty good job considering I'd put up an out of office in my email, dodged calls from Nan and even jammed a chair in front of my door so Evelyn couldn't let herself in. I considered turning off my phone, but I was still holding out hope that Leith would come back—that he'd text me or call Will or *something*. And I'd hate myself forever if I missed it.

My phone lit up again—Mom this time.

"What," I answered.

"That's a way to greet a mother," she sniffed into the phone.

"That's a way to greet a saboteur."

"Caoimhe, I've already told you I'm sorry—"

"Are you calling for a reason?" She'd told Leith he could come with us, but it didn't make up for trying a new avenue for pressuring me into leaving Boston. Joke was on her, it just made me dig my heels in harder. Or maybe I *was* being difficult.

"I've got tickets to Dublin," she said.

Maybe not.

"Bon voyage," I said, groping around on the couch for the last unopened bag of Crunchy Crispy Cheesys.

"Caoimhe, please," she said. "You can't possibly want to stay here now the whole city is on monster watch."

"I'm also on monster watch," I said, pumping a fist in the air when I found the bag. Popping it open I crammed several in my mouth. The man I loved was in incredible danger, lost at sea, maybe never to return, and I was shunning the rest of my family. But at least I had salty cheese bites. "That means I'm with my people. Monster watchers for life."

My front door gave a rattling shake and then a thud before keys jangled in the lock. It didn't open more than a slit but this time it wasn't Eve interrupting my phone call.

"Miss Ryan," came Pete's voice muffled through the door. Had I missed an inspection notice?

"Oh shit, gotta go Mom." I hung up on her protest, leaping off the couch and dragging the chair away. I pulled the door open to face Pete, staring at me in all his four foot glory. I swore his mole was even bigger than last time—definitely hairier.

"We need to speak, Miss Ryan," he said. I frantically racked my brain for a missed rent check or another fire-alarm incident. Nothing came to mind. "I understand you have a connection to the creature that was seen in the harbor last week."

"I don't know what—"

"Come with me, Miss Ryan. There are some folk you need to meet." Before I could ask any questions, he was plodding down the stairs, his hands clasped behind him politely, leaving me to follow in my filthy sweats and baggy hoodie.

We wound down into the basement, stopping in front of the laundry machines in the all-brick dank room. Pete took out a keyring I'd never seen before, made of twining green twigs. A single golden key hung from it and I rubbed my eyes to make sure I was seeing it right—it was in the shape of a harp.

Pete plucked the pretend strings on the harp and a few small notes sounded. The bricks in front of us ground against each other as they shifted in the wall, revealing a hidden doorway and a set of stone steps that led further down.

He started down these steps but I hesitated. When I could no longer see him, his voice floated up from the darkness.

"Do not be afraid, Miss Ryan." I took a deep breath and followed.

The darkness was thick and I couldn't see more than an inch or so in front of my face. It made for slow going as I braced myself on either side of the tiny stairwell, feeling the walls for stability.

If I got to the bottom of this just to be eaten by my troll of a landlord I was going to be so—

I stepped suddenly into a room filled with soft glowing lanterns. Plush fabric hung from the ceiling and a delicately embroidered tapestry covered the back wall. A large round table made from deep magenta wood was in the center of the room and as my eyes adjusted to the light, I could make out the figures seated there. Pete was standing near the head, and he gestured to the seat nearest the entrance I'd come through.

"Join us," he said.

It was all very vampiric—I couldn't wait to tell Eve. I pulled out the heavy wooden seat, noticing the ornate carvings along the arms of various fruits and flowers. The cushion was dusty but not uncomfortable as I sat down.

"So, you have more than the four tenants I've met, huh?" My voice echoed off the walls and bounced back to me, thin and scared. I wasn't fooling anyone, not even the reverb.

"Miss Ryan," a new voice came from the head of the table. A thin-faced man with a gaunt complexion leaned into the light. "We have been watching you for some time."

"Not creepy." I tried to use sarcasm to feel better. It wasn't working.

"We know what you are, Duchess," said a voice like the wind through leaves. A shimmering grey shape to my right caught the light but no matter how I squinted I couldn't make out who was speaking. "You belong with us."

"You're all making this sound like a cult." A square fist slammed the table and I jumped. A stout red-headed woman with bright eyes and a full, lush beard was sitting next to the gaunt man at the head. She looked vaguely familiar but I couldn't put my finger on it. She turned to me and smiled, the gesture spreading up to her crinkling eyes and apple cheeks. "I'm Wilamena," she said. "And I run the—"

"Savvy Squirrel!" The cafe by the harbor was notorious for its delicious seasonal coffees and addictive pastries. No one could figure out what made their treats so much better than everyone else's.

"You've heard of me," she preened her beard, pleased.

"Your cafe has a line out the door every Sunday morning. It's impossible to get the croissants before they're gone. That's you?"

She nodded. "I'll tell you now, it's an ancient dwarven recipe," she winked. "I won't share the secret but I'll save you a croissant next weekend."

"Dwarven..." It dawned on me as I looked from Wilamena to the gaunt-faced man to the shimmering form next to me.

"Pete," I started. "You said we had 'folk' to meet." How had I missed that? In all his formalities, why didn't the casual language stick out?

"And he meant it," the gaunt faced man said. "I am Patrick, head chairman of the Boston Harbor Small Business Association, which is better known to those seated here as the Boston Unusualities Society."

"He's a vampire," Wilamena winked at me.

"We don't need to play Baby's First Monster Reveal, Mena." Another woman with shaggy black hair sticking out at all angles and a square jaw entered from behind me, taking the seat to my other side.

"Says the werewolf." Wilamena grinned, pleased with herself. The other woman rolled her eyes.

"I'm Roxanne." She waved and I noticed her fingers ended in long black nails sharpened to a point.

"You're late," Patrick chided and Roxanne bared her teeth. "Back to the business at hand." He turned to me and steepled his fingers together.

"We'd like to invite you to join our Board. We've heard of your prowess as a publicity agent but also of your incredible powers for luck. We believe we can offer you the support you seek here in Boston in exchange for your occasional professional services."

"Sorry, what?"

"We'll help you find your boyfriend if you write us a few press releases once and again." Roxanne looked under her long nails, bored.

"You know Leith?" I didn't bother correcting the boyfriend moniker. If he ever came back, I was going to keep him as long as he'd let me, which I figured made him more than my boyfriend anyway. My heart stuttered back to life after several days of grieving. If anyone could find a merman in Boston it was a roomful of magical folk.

"We don't 'know' him exactly, though I saw him in the cafe last week with another of you lucky gals," said Wilamena. "They were having a real heated conversation before they left."

"My mom," I said.

"Ah, is the other leprechaun still here?" The shimmering form next to me shivered.

I shook my head. "Not for much longer," I said. "She doesn't think it's safe here. Too many humans."

The room exchanged a look around me and I felt like I was missing something.

"We are partly to blame for that," said Pete.

"What do you mean?"

"I fear we have let one another fend for themselves for far too long," Patrick chimed in. "We should have gathered long before anything unfortunate could occur."

"So you heard," I said. I was unsure if I should feel angry or not.

"We are sorry for the loss of your father," Patrick said, his voice soft and regretful. "But it was his passing that prompted our unification efforts. We can no longer afford to operate independently of one another and new alliances must be forged."

I looked away from the eyes at the table, searching the dramatically draped ceiling for an answer. No, I wasn't angry. I was exhausted. And lonely.

"You'll find Leith?"

Patrick nodded. "We will do everything we can to bring him back safely."

"And then help him stay safe," Wilamena added. "Both of you."

"How?"

"We each have unique talents that when brought together create a more effective force at staying hidden from humans," Patrick explained.

"I don't want to be hidden," I said. "Not from everyone." I thought about Eve and a pang of regret hit my heart. I promised myself silently that I'd call her as soon as I left the extra basement.

"Provided you keep the truth of our Association from your human companions, we do not care what you tell them about yourselves," Patrick said.

"I have three human boyfriends," Wilamena shot me another wink. "They all have fantasy women fetishes so that's how we met. It's cute how they bond over it, actually."

"It was two last time I saw you," Roxanne said, leaning across the table to give Wilamena a hearty high five.

"So?" Pete asked from next to Patrick.

I nodded. "I'm in." If it would bring back Leith and keep him safe, I would've signed over my first born to a strange man in the woods—never mind how much I'd been warned explicitly against doing that.

The room clapped politely and Pete nodded to me.

"We will have the appropriate agreement drawn up," Patrick said. "And Roxanne will begin searching for your Leith tonight."

Hope flooded my system and I felt my entire body begin to relax. Leith could finally come home. And when he did, I would never let him go again.

***

"So you're *not* dead?" Evelyn Sharp was angry.

"Will you let me buy you lunch and explain myself?"

"Only so I can make sure it's actually Caoimhe on the phone right now and not some other monster lurking in Boston."

Neither of us laughed.

We picked the usual—a French place downtown that was ridiculously expensive for dinner but had the same food for cheap at lunch. We called it Hacks, but never to their face, and we kept going back because they put drugs in the fries—seriously, I never had a better French fry in the city.

Eve was there when I arrived, arms crossed, scowling at a mid-day cocktail. Before I could so much as open my mouth, she leapt up from the table and crushed me in a vise-like hug.

"Don't you ever disappear on me like that again Caoimhe Ryan," she hissed. "I will kill you if you aren't already dead."

"I'm sorry," I whispered back, comforted to the point of tears by the smell of her luxury perfume mixed with something vaguely musty. "Did you not wash this coat when you bought it?"

"If people don't know it's vintage from a mile away, then why did I spend five hours digging through Goodwill for it." Her voice stayed low, kept that same ferocity, and I let myself huff out a laugh.

Evelyn loved me as much as she loved a vintage treasure. Which meant she probably loved me more than she loved herself.

Finally, she let me go and gestured to the booth so we could sit next to each other. "I already ordered fries and two lamb burgers. You're going to tell me everything from start to finish."

"Shouldn't you be telling *me* everything?" I asked. It had only been a few days but it felt like years.

She heaved a sigh and rolled her eyes dramatically. "I fake dated a merman so my best friend would be more open to love but accidentally tricked myself into falling in love instead and had the most mind-blowing sex of my entire life." She sipped her cocktail nonchalantly and smacked her lips for effect. "Same old, same old. Your turn."

"*What!*" The waiter approaching our table did an abrupt one-eighty.

"Please, like you didn't see that coming from a mile away."

"Not even from an inch away, explain yourself."

"What's to explain?" She shrugged. "You obviously had the hots for Leith but you were never gonna do anything about it without a push and you *never* take my advice after that whole kombucha incident— "

"Gee I can't imagine why."

She leveled a finger at me. "Forgiveness is the foundation of friendship, C." The waiter returned, setting a plate of perfectly crisp golden fries in front of us with a flourish. "Anyway, I knew I had to lead by example and Will is a smoke show— "

"He was so drunk he couldn't stand when you met."

"Oh yeah, that was the first part of our agreement. He needed to hop right up on that wagon because I was not about to be cleaning puke out of my wardrobe just so you could get laid. But that doesn't matter right now."

She gestured with a fry, chomping happily. "It worked better than I planned when you called me that day all jealous— "

"Concerned about your safety! I thought he was going to eat you!"

She waggled her eyebrows at me and took another bite of her fry.

"*For dinner* Evelyn, not oral sex." The waiter holding our burgers hesitated and I waved him over. We waited in silence while he practically dropped the plates in front of us and scurried away.

"Whatever," she waved her hands like she could scatter my words through the air. "You called me all pissed, I got to tell you to learn to trust in a way that I *knew* you would hear because we were fighting and then you did it!"

"You manipulated me into going on a date with Leith because you knew I'd be concerned about your safety?" My voice was shrill beyond even customer service octaves. My stomach flipped and the burger in front of me suddenly didn't seem all that appetizing.

"God no, C, who do you think I am? I was going to go the 'look how happy I am you should try it' route but instead you came in all Joan of Arc triumphant ready to break us up so I had to counterattack. That's all."

"You're insane," I whispered, staring at my best friend.

"Duh," she said, lifting her burger and biting in happily. She chewed in blissful silence for a few minutes. "But you wouldn't love me if I wasn't."

I sighed and sat in the overwhelm washing over my body for a moment. My nerves were so exhausted they were no longer strung tight, they were simply slack in my body, leaving me feeling floaty and disconnected.

"Besides," she said around a mouthful of burger. "By the time you called me freaked out, I really was happy with Will. We started talking about dating seriously after that and here we are."

"What if I didn't go out with Leith?"

She shrugged and took another bite of burger in answer. "But you did."

I looked down at my plate and decided my own burger was too much challenge at the moment. I reached for another fry instead.

"Speaking of," Eve set hers down and wiped her hands on a napkin. "How are you holding up?"

I took a breath. "Better now," I said. "I met some people who are going to help me find him."

"Who?"

I hesitated.

"Hey," Eve snapped, her voice cutting the air between us. "Don't do that. No more secrets, C."

I nodded. They did say I could tell her. But I couldn't risk someone eavesdropping and exposing the BUS. I pulled out my phone and used the same trick Eve and I used when we were in a loud club and wanted to gossip about the hot guy at the bar. I typed furiously before holding the screen up. I watched Eve's eyes scan the screen as she read, her eyes growing wider and wider. By the end, her jaw was slack and I could see her half-chewed burger.

"Absolutely *insane*," she said around her food.

"Close your mouth."

She stuck her tongue out to show me her food then swallowed. Gross.

"So…this…association," she made air quotes with her fingers. "What're they gonna do, hunt him down?"

"Not in a threatening way," I said, thinking immediately of how nervous Roxanne made me. "But basically, yeah."

"And what are you gonna do?"

I shrugged, hating the answer as it formed. "Wait."

Eve nodded and picked up her own phone, tapping to make a call.

"Hey sweet pea," she said into it. "I'm gonna need you to run to the store and get a few stuffed crust pepperoni pizzas and one of those Caesar salad kits in the bag." She paused. "Yes, the bag is for you." Another pause. "Because we both know you ate all the leftover kettle corn from the carnival already and whatever other garbage for lunch." She winked at me and I squinted back.

"And we'll need two bags of chips, one of each traditional flavor, and a few pints of ice cream, dealer's choice." She paused again. "Yeah." Another pause, longer this time. "She says all she can do is wait, so that's what we're gonna do with her." She nodded into the phone for a few moments before making kissing noises into it and hanging up.

"Will is coming over after work since he's off before me, and I'll be over right after," she said. "I'll have to see if I can get someone to cover the student showcase at MassArt for me tonight."

A lot of things hit me all at once—relief that I wasn't going to be alone in a strange purgatory, hope that everything would be okay, joy at how the truth of my life was playing out in real-time and I could see the wheels catching in grooves as if they'd been made to fit. I didn't want to cry in public, especially not when I already looked like a hot wreck in a French restaurant with my untouched burger, but it was happening.

Eve squeezed my hand from across the table. "We'll get through this, C," she said. "And Leith will come home to you. I promise."

I nodded, squeezing her hand back.

"Not now, obviously, but at some point, we need to discuss your whole mini-to-jumbo trick. I'm not letting you off the hook for that one just because you're a little traumatized right now."

I laughed, wiping my face off and trying to swallow the knot in my throat.

"Are you like that all the time and I'm just seeing an illusion?" She asked. "Because your hand at least feels the right size. Does your lepre-coochie adjust accordingly?"

"My *what*."

"Lepre-coochie," she repeated as if she was asking about my bum knee and not my vagina. "Leprechaun coochie."

"You're right," I said laughing and picking up my burger. "We're not gonna discuss that right now."

FROM MISTER FLIPPER FOR IMMEDIATE RELEASE

Boston, MA. Mister Flipper and the Boston Harbor Small Business Association (BHSBA) stand in solidarity with the maligned Mister Flipper employee who was spotted rescuing a small child at yesterday's carnival.

Guests at the first-ever annual Very Well Boston and Mister Flipper Customer Appreciation Carnival witnessed what may have seemed like an inexplicable appearance of an unidentified creature. Many eyewitness accounts are circulating online claiming to have seen a sea monster or a "merman" rescue a young boy who fell into the water along the docks during the carnival.

The reality is that the child was rescued by a Mister Flipper employee with a rare genetic skin condition that causes fish-like appearances when the adrenal gland is activated. At Mister Flipper, we invite differences all aboard—each unique individual can contribute something different to the ship—and we ask the city of Boston and our community to do the same.

"The Boston Harbor Small Business Association stands with Leith Riordan of Mister Flipper in support of his unique condition that he brings to work every day," said Patrick Aglio, Chairman of the BHSBA. "There are countless others who must do the same and it is unjust to expect them to work in fear every day of being ridiculed and mocked."

Riordan will return to work after a few mental health days. We ask guests to respect his privacy at this time.

22

Leith

The first rays of morning light ignited the dust motes in the air sending cold sparks through Kelly's darkened office.

I rolled over from my spot on the floor and stared at the stained ceiling. I'd only been here one night, and it already felt like taking the coward's way out. I should've stayed in the ocean—should've stayed away.

But Boston and Caoimhe were calling.

I could feel them pulling in my gut the same way I felt the call of the open ocean, singing to me that I belonged out among the waves, feeding and swimming without a care. Now, it was Caoimhe my instincts called to.

Unfortunately, instincts have no common sense.

I ran a hand over my face and found the world was still there when I opened my eyes.

The one thing I always dreaded happening had happened. I'd been found out. And despite all my emergency planning and exit strategies, I still couldn't leave. I always said if the humans discovered me, I'd just go somewhere else—or give up living among humans forever. It could only have been temporary anyway since we all knew from the stories that secret identities always come to the surface given enough time.

What I never planned on was falling in love—with a city and a woman. And I had no contingencies. I never planned anything past leaving because I never thought I'd be unable to leave.

Now I was stuck in an in-between space, unwilling to run away, unable to stay, stuck in an office hovering above the water as neither land nor sea.

Kelly nearly obliterated me when I crawled up the ladder leading to her office from the water.

"You better call Caoimhe," she said before handing me the keys and leaving. She didn't say anything about the stacks of coffee cups littered all over the office or the fact that she was still "working" at ten p.m. A pang hit my heart when I realized I didn't want to leave Kelly or Will behind either. I could live a hundred lifetimes in the ocean and never have friends like them again.

Of course I'd lost my phone and didn't have Caoimhe's number memorized—I hadn't had time.

I sat up, feeling a stiff pain screaming in my lower back at sleeping on the lumpy floor. Normally by now I'd hear the familiar quick footsteps of Kelly coming to unlock the office, a steaming cup of coffee in hand, her cellphone pinched between her cheek and her shoulder as she booked one school group or another. The dock next to us would be a flurry of morning activity as our neighbors readied for their own daily work.

But it was silent.

How had our lives been knocked so far sideways in such a short amount of time?

Caoimhe was probably worried sick. I thought about going to her apartment a million times, stopping myself short of crawling from the water to do just that when I remembered the chaos of the crowd on the rooftop—and that was just when I was a so-called internet celebrity.

I didn't want to bring strangers to her door. Not when it would also bring danger to her life.

For the million-and-first time, I thought about leaving without saying goodbye to keep her safe, to keep her away from prying eyes, internet fiends, and kidnapping researchers. I thought about slipping away into the water and never returning, allowing the fervor to blow over for the ones I cared for most. They, at least, could return to their lives if I wasn't here. Not immediately, but they could.

The office phone rang, startling me back to my own buzzing skin. I groaned, shaking off the stiffness in my limbs, and half-crawled to the desk to pick it up.

"I'm on my way in, don't be naked," Kelly barked into the phone. I grunted in response before hanging up and immediately grabbing the spare pants I'd slept in.

If I *did* stay, I was going to have to replenish Kelly's thoughtful spare clothing stash. I'd run off with two pairs of pants and one shirt now, leaving the cabinet sparse.

If I *did* stay.

The thought whirled around like a tornado caught in a mason jar, slamming against the inside of my head with barely contained violence.

The art gallery openings and literary readings I could see. I could take Caoimhe to my favorite wing of the art museum. I could watch Will fall in love with Evelyn, the shadows of his drowned senses gone from under his eyes as he learned to swim again—as he learned to be his entire self with another person.

I thought about Caoimhe falling asleep on my shoulder, her legs kicked up across my lap while Will and Evelyn flirted on the couch next to us. The warmth and comfort of that night was enough to make me forsake the ocean entirely.

And if my instincts were calling out for this new home, then I'd always be pulled back anyway. Fear slammed through me, fast and icy, as I realized that leaving—whether to protect the others or myself—was no longer an option. I would always end up back here. Nature and my heart would make sure of it.

The office suddenly felt too small, like a cage with rapidly shrinking bars. I needed out.

A ridiculous bucket hat with a wide brim hung above Kelly's desk with the Mister Flipper's logo stitched on it—a failed merchandising attempt from the early days. I grabbed it and a pair of novelty beer sunglasses from a dusty shelf, cramming both on my head and slipping into a pair of flip-flops by the door. I checked my shirtless reflection in the window—I looked ridiculous, but nothing like myself.

Kelly would be pissed I snuck out, so I decided to burn off my anxiety by walking to the Savvy Squirrel. If she beat me back to the office, I could soothe the savage beast with apple crisp macchiatos. If I beat her, then she couldn't be mad at me for asking for another day on the office floor while I tried to make a decision about my next move.

No one paid me any mind as I walked along the harbor. In fact, the only thing anyone seemed to be looking at that morning was the water. A few die-hards in thick coats were camped out in folding chairs, coolers stacked next to them, cameras with long lenses balanced on railings.

The detritus of the monster-hunting fervor from the last few days was all around me. I sidestepped homemade signs with blurry photos of my mershark form printed across it, of cheaply made mermaid toys dropped and crushed to the ground.

One sign stopped me as I neared the cafe, flapping on the ground near a gutter. It was drawn in red crayon, the letters tall and uneven.

"Come back," it said. "We luv u Mr. Merman."

I stared for what was probably a suspicious amount of time, trying to reconcile what I was seeing with the memory of the screaming boy's face at the carnival.

A paper coffee cup suddenly obstructed my vision. I followed the gloved hand clamped around it up to the kindly bearded face of a bright-eyed woman with long red hair. She was wearing a brilliant shade of purple lipstick that made her red mustache sparkle.

"Go on," she said. "Take it. And don't worry, I brought one for your friend as well." She held up another cup, this one carefully stoppered to keep the steam from leaking away into the crisp morning air.

I took the cup, savoring the warmth against my palms. I hadn't realized how cold it was until that moment and I shivered in my t-shirt.

"Do I know you?" I asked. Something about her seemed comfortable in a way that made me think I should recognize her. But there was no way I'd forget a woman with a beard that well-maintained.

She shook her head. "But I know you," she said with a wink.

Fear trilled down my back, calling a warning. She must've recognized it on my face because she held a hand up in peace.

"No, no," she said. "Not like that. Like this." And she reached up to push her hair away from the side of her face, revealing one delicately pointed ear ringed with gold piercings.

"You're…" I glanced from her face to her feet and back again. "I give up."

"Wilamena," she said. "The owner of the Savvy Squirrel. And a dwarf." She mouthed the final word, a warm smile splitting her face as realization dawned across mine.

"I knew those croissants were too good to be human," I said.

"Caoimhe said the same thing."

Her name from this stranger's mouth nearly made me drop my coffee and I found myself gripping Wilamena's arm with a deep need.

"Is she ok? Does she know I had to lay low for her own safety? Can you tell her for me, please, I—" The words slammed out of me faster than I could think about what I was saying, but Wilamena simply shrugged off my hand, looping the free arm around my shoulder and steering me back toward the dock.

"I'll do you one better," she said. "I'll take you to her. But first, I'd like us to have a little chat with your siren friend."

***

I tried to remember to breathe as Wilamena and Kelly both walked on either side of me, chatting amicably. Kelly returned to the office with my own clothes, a less conspicuous hat, and a pair of normal sunglasses. She gushed over Wilamena so much that there wasn't time for her to berate me for leaving the office alone.

Apparently, Mister Flipper closed for a few days while Kelly and Will figured out what to do about the insanity I caused at the carnival. Kelly showed me the press release that Caoimhe had written and then released on behalf of Mister Flipper and the Boston Harbor Small Business Association—the latter of which was apparently responsible for the amulet now safely tied around my neck.

"It's charmed so that human sight will gloss right over you," Wilamena explained as she handed me the small brown stone.

"So I'm invisible?"

"No," she said, smiling. "Just not as visible as you have been lately."

I didn't have to wear it all the time—or even for the long term. But the BUS—the Boston Unusualities Society and the real name of the Small Business Association—would prefer that I wore it until the monster fervor died down.

All that meant in the moment was that Kelly and Wilamena could have a friendly chat as we walked down the street and all anyone would look at was Wilamena's beard. And plenty of people were looking at her beard. I wasn't so sure with it on display I would even need the amulet.

"Bearded women exist among humans," she said in response to something Kelly asked. I hadn't been listening as we turned the corner onto Caoimhe's street. "And it's my best feature, so why would I hide it

176

under a glamor if I don't have to?"

"It just seems like a lot of attention," Kelly said.

"And yet, it's still less than I deserve," Wilamena said with a put-upon sigh.

I hesitated in front of the door to Caoimhe's building, watching Kelly and Wilamena take the steps quickly. Kelly turned back around and put a hand on her hip.

"Don't bitch out now," she said.

Wilamena put a soft hand on her shoulder. "Maybe go see what Pete has made for breakfast. He makes a killer quiche I'd hate for you to miss when it's still warm."

"Is that your way of telling me to butt out?" Kelly arched an eyebrow at her new friend.

"Of course not," Wilamena put a hand on her chest like she was insulted, but her smile was teasing. "It's my way of telling you to let a man be nervous when he reunites with the love of his life and to seriously not miss a hot slice of quiche. Now get." She smacked Kelly's shoulder sharply but affectionately and Kelly squeaked before scooting in the door.

Once Kelly was across the threshold, the dwarf woman turned to me.

"Thank you," I said. "For everything."

"You're welcome," she said, raising her coffee cup in a cheers. "Now seriously, don't bitch out." She threw me a wink and stepped inside, leaving me alone on the sidewalk.

23

Caoimhe

I could see him frozen on the sidewalk below.

"What's he waiting for?" Will whispered over my shoulder. He and Evelyn had been camped out in my living room for the last two days, feeding me a steady stream of junk food and campy monster movies.

I watched Leith's stormy face scan the front of my building. A strange brown stone on a simple cord hung around his neck but otherwise he looked exactly the same. It was as if the last week hadn't happened at all and my heart was still pounding on the boardwalk as I waited for him to respond to my stupid jokes.

But this *was* different. Because I was not going to wait this time.

I had waited long enough—to be free of secrets, to be myself with the ones I loved.

Without thinking, I spun on my heel and sprinted for the door.

"You're going in that?" Eve called after me as I took the stairs two at a time. There wasn't time to change out of my fluffy pajama pants with snacking sloths or the ancient boy band tour t-shirt I'd clung to since high school.

I threw open the first front door, leaving only the storm screen and the mud room between me and Leith. Before I could cross the threshold, Leith opened the last door and looked at me, first startled, then relieved as I watched a full smile spread across his face, crinkling up around his brilliant grey eyes.

We greeted each other in a sudden, frantic flurry of cross talk.

"I'm sorry—"

"You're late—"

"I wanted to come sooner—"

"Where have you been?"

Leith reached a hand to my face, sliding calloused fingers into my hair and pulling me into him for a kiss. I let myself melt into it, feeling warm joy bloom in my chest. Something low and hot sprung to life in my core, tightening with need, desperate to have more of the man I loved and had nearly lost.

Leith pulled away and I let out a small, disappointed noise despite myself.

"I'm sorry," he said.

"Yeah, you said that already."

"But I need you to know it," his face was serious. "I would've come to you immediately but I didn't want to put you in any danger because of my…" He looked up at the ceiling like the words he wanted were there.

"Your paparazzi entourage?" I finished for him. He nodded, giving me a shy half smile. "I've lived in Boston my entire life and the only people who know I'm a leprechaun are the people upstairs in my apartment—and this new local group I'm joining."

"The BUS?"

"Oh right, you walked up with Wilamena." I watched him toy with the stone around his neck. Up close I could see it was a dull brown, with no sheen or glint to it, but the surface was intricately carved with swirling floral motifs. "What's the necklace for?"

"It's why I could finally come here," he said.

"You say that like you were away at war for years," I tried to joke. It really had felt that way—like I was endlessly waiting for my love to return when he was in grave danger.

"I missed you," he said, planting a kiss on my forehead.

"You didn't answer my question, really," I said, tapping a finger to the necklace.

"It lets me hide in plain sight," he said. "Humans just glance right over me like I'm not there."

"God, I'm glad I'm not a human." And that had to be the first time in my life I'd ever felt that way. But I meant it. I was finally glad to be entirely myself and it was Leith and Evelyn and Will who had given me the guts to settle into that self—they had given me a safe place to land after years of flying below the radar.

A rumbly throat cleared behind us. I turned to see Pete holding a steaming quiche pan in my hand, his other arm looped through Kelly's.

"You two are causing a fire hazard," he said. "And Miss Nerida needs to be escorted home."

We stepped out into the morning light, letting Kelly and Pete make their way past us.

"Needs to be escorted?" Leith asked, face slack in disbelief. Kelly shot him a look before turning back to Pete and smiling wide. It was a total transformation and I realized I'd never seen her fully smile. She looked younger, like years of worry were suddenly erased by one simple expression. A light danced in her eyes as she pressed herself a little closer to Pete. We watched them go, both of us in a confused daze.

"Come with me," I said, shaking my head to clear it. "I have something I want to show you."

Upstairs, Will and Evelyn nowhere to be seen, I tapped quickly on my phone before handing it to Leith and then busied myself in the kitchen. I grabbed my trusty pot, filling it with water and steel cut oats before setting it to boil with the lid. I leaned against the counter, glancing between the pot and Leith's quickly transforming face as he read the social media search I'd pulled up.

"I can't believe it," he said.

"Believe it." I searched it myself last night when my sleepless brain kicked into work mode. I was curious what the general public sentiment was about their "supposed merman." The results had surprised me. Not because I thought the people of Boston were so cruel they would continue to harass a "hard worker with an unfortunate and untreatable skin condition" as I'd written in the press release, but because of the joy and excitement Leith had apparently inspired.

There was video after video of kids diving into beds, screaming "I'm a merman!" People were using #MermanInTheStreets to flirt with one another in creative ways. And my personal favorite was the #ImAMerman threads, filled with people sharing the ways they'd been isolated by society because of their differences only to find their own community regardless. There were stories of Dungeons and Dragon groups celebrating life-long friendships and marriages, of model train enthusiasts attending conventions for the first time, and something called "furries" which I had never heard of but seemed to be the happiest of them all.

Leith looked up at me, face slack, eyes wide, as I stirred the now finished oats in the pot. I dished them between two bowls, adding in heaping spoonfuls of brown sugar and sliced almonds. Then pulled the secret ingredient from the top of the fridge—Irish whiskey. I poured a shot into each bowl and stirred again, handing one bowl to Leith.

"How did you do this?" He asked, holding up the phone. I shrugged.

"Some things you don't need magic for, you just need humanity." I clinked my bowl to his and grinned. "Slainte."

"Incredible," Leith said around mouthfuls of oatmeal and I hummed happily in agreement. "You're incredible."

I swallowed and laughed. "I didn't do anything," I said. "The recipe isn't even mine."

He shook his head. "The press release you wrote, waiting for me while I was getting my head straight." He looked at me like I was a hidden masterpiece, freshly painted, never revealed to the world. "And now showing me all this?" He pointed to the phone again. "You're something else, Caoimhe," he said.

"So I've been told," I grinned over my bowl.

"And I can't believe how lucky I am to love you."

My heart stuttered to a stop.

"To what?" I asked. I set down my oatmeal so I wouldn't drop it as my hands started shaking.

"To love you," he said, closing the distance between us and wrapping his arms around me. "I love you, Caoimhe."

"I love you, too," I breathed, suddenly aware of how natural and easy it felt to say it. It had been sitting there in my chest this whole time and finally speaking it out loud felt like releasing a flood of water from behind a dam. It was overwhelming and terrifying, but beautiful as it settled between us, glistening in the sun.

"Blech," came a tiny voice from above us.

"Fucking fairies," I said against Leith's lips. He kissed me once, gentle and light before whispering back.

"I know where they can't find us."

***

The water was surprisingly calm along the beach of the harbor island. A clear sky sparkled a brilliant blue across the waves. Leith and I lay basking in the solitude, hand in webbed hand, his tail flopping occasionally in the shallow water. He'd brought me out to one of his favorite places, letting me ride on his back while he swam. He was built like an expert predator, and the sheer size of him was overwhelming at first. But I knew he was still Leith—still the man I loved and who loved me.

182

Looking over his true form, speckled with brown and white spots, I was hit again with an overwhelming sense of gratitude for the people who had helped us to finally feel like we could be entirely ourselves in the only city we could imagine calling home. Without the amulet—and by extension its adjustable cord that looped easily around both our heads—we couldn't enjoy this easy time together. Without the BUS, Leith couldn't have come home to me so easily.

And without Will's meddling, I would never have stepped foot on the docks setting this whole thing in motion in the first place.

Leith tugged on my arm, interrupting my thoughts. I looked up to see him gazing down at me, this time a heated mischief in his normally tender gaze.

"You're blocking the sun, buddy," I teased.

He gave me an exaggerated frown before wiggling his non-existent eyebrows and tugging on my arm again.

"Okay, okay," I said sitting up to meet him so that the cord stayed looped around us both. Ships still came by the islands at various points in the day and I didn't want to risk yet another period of loneliness because Leith had been sighted again. "Where are we going now?"

I slipped myself free of the amulet as Leith pushed himself back into the water, following his massive, athletic form in the water. His tail cut the waves like a weapon and a thrill ran down my spine at the way my instincts railed against my following him. Of course Leith would never hurt me—or anyone, for that matter. But the shape of him suggested otherwise and something primal in the back of my mind screamed as I let him take my hands and pull me further from the shore.

Once we were deep enough in the water that I could see Leith treading water comfortably, I looped the cord back over my neck, giving us both protection and privacy from the rest of the world. Here it was just us—hidden from everyone but one another.

I kissed Leith then, kicking my legs slowly in the water and clinging on to his muscled arms to keep from being swallowed by the waves. In this form, his mouth was flat but not unpleasant, and although he didn't have a tongue to chase with my own, his teeth had grown thicker and sharper. He nipped quickly at my top lip, igniting a heat between my legs that threatened dangerous things in deep water.

"Are we trying to have a Guillermo Del Toro moment?" I asked.

In answer, Leith pushed the straps of my swimsuit down with one hand, the other clasped firmly around my waist. He set his shark teeth onto the tender skin of my neck and shoulders, peppering it with small bites that sent shocks of pleasure through my entire body.

"I read online that sharks explore the world by biting," I said, breathless even though I'd stopped treading water, wrapping my legs to rest on Leith's tail as he kept us afloat. It was smooth beneath my feet and I could feel the muscles working in the water. "How curious are you?"

Leith looked up at me then, gaze burning a hole into my soul before shoving my swimsuit top down to my waist. I gasped as the cold water shocked my tight nipples and I closed my eyes to fully absorb the sensation. Quickly, short, sharp bites were on my breasts and then my nipples, making me arch up and out of the water.

Well, that was one way of answering the question.

Need made me clench, and I was painfully aware of how achingly empty I was.

"Leith, please," I begged as his free hand found the waistline of my swimsuit bottoms. He pushed these down too, exposing my hot, tight pussy to the water and I gasped at the cold slap of water against it. He teased a single finger up and through my slick folds, finding my clit and circling it a few times. The water no longer felt too cold as waves of heat slammed through me.

I ground against his hand, seeking something more fulfilling as he teased and flicked my clit. I felt the start of a finger at my opening but it didn't venture far. I pulled away and looked at Leith. He lifted his free hand out of the water and showed it to me, fingers splayed out to reveal the webbing at that connected each finger at the second joint.

That wasn't going to get inside me.

I leaned my head against his shoulder and blew an exasperated sigh into the water. Leith tapped my shoulder to get my attention, face questioning.

"If you have a solution that doesn't drown us," I said. "I'll happily try it."

I was so turned on I'd let him fuck me with an octopus tentacle if that's what it took. The thought only emphasized how empty my cunt was. I'd have to investigate that kink later.

Leith nodded, planting a no-lipped smooch on my cheek and then scooped my ass firmly in both hands. He returned to my breasts, nipping lightly at them until the need rose again to a crescendo within me. I was about to start searching for a tentacle myself when something soft and puckered latched onto my clit, sucking me into a sudden, sharp, blinding orgasm. I leaned my head down into the water so my scream was swallowed by the depths and didn't attract attention from onlookers.

Before I could fully recover, a second soft, fleshy tendril found my entrance while the first was still wrapped gently around my throbbing, sensitive clit. The second tendril began to snake inside of me, the head of it pressing against my walls.

I looked down to see both tendrils snaking from Leith, attached to a lower part of his tail. His eyes were hooded in pleasure, his face tight with effort. A muscle ticked in his jaw and I kissed where it feathered under his skin. The tendril answered by widening within me and I moaned as I stretched to accommodate it.

The first tendril let go of my clit and slid in next to the second. They both began to widen against my walls before pumping in and out of me alternately, first one and then immediately the other slamming up and into me, driving me back up toward the edge where I would meet oblivion.

One tendril began to twist within me, spinning its flat head against my walls and finding the spot that made my entire body arch and tense as I rocked my hips against it, desperate for release. The other tendril slid free, wrapping around my clit again, and sucking aggressively. The tendril inside me pressed and spun and slammed into me and the dual sensations soon had me riding up and over the edge, coming a second time in yet another screaming orgasm that had me pressing my face, breathless into the water to release it.

When I literally came up for air, everything was warm and hazy, lulled by the current, and I felt Leith continue to thrust rapidly for a few blissful, desperate moments until I watched him open his mouth in a silent moan.

We clung to each other in the water, floating there for I don't know how long, until I felt Leith carefully adjust my swimsuit and push me onto his back. I clung on, letting the current and his strength carry my spent form back to the Boston shore.

I opened my eyes to the familiar walls of the Mister Flipper office, snuggled into a pile of blankets and clothes that smelled like Leith and the sea. Before I could acclimate, the door flung open and Eve came screaming into the room, scrambling into the pile with me.

"Oh my god, you have to see this!" She had her phone open to a news article with a massive photo of a runway model covered in glittering scales. "Balenciaga has launched a new mermaid line of menswear!"

I looked to the door to see Leith standing just inside the door, Will leaning in over his shoulder.

"We've made it to the runway, baby!" Evelyn kicked her legs in the air from where she was lying next to me, looking like an overly excited cat with a mouse. "A whole runway show for mermen! And I've got four seats, front row in New York City. You're all coming with me. How fucking lucky are we?"

I caught Leith's eyes by the door and felt a grin split my entire face. "Absolutely the luckiest."

The End

24

Epilogue

One month later...

I shifted in the hard plastic seat, gripping my coffee mug and checking my phone for the thousandth time. Overhead, a crisp, polite female voice announced yet another flight's departure. Next to me, Leith put a heavy hand on my knee.

"Stop," he said gently.

"I can't," I said, shifting again and bouncing his hand off. "I *hate* flying."

"You were just fine on the way to New York."

"Yeah, I was *drunk*." Our trip to see the exclusive merman line walk the runway with Eve and Will had been a whirlwind of interviews, photo-ops, and haute couture gifts that left us all a little dazed and giddy. I'd crushed my plane anxiety with a little weed and a lot of alcohol.

"So, get drunk," Leith flipped a page of the massive tome on the Irish stained glass artist Harry Clarke he had settled in his lap.

"With my mom?" I arched my eyebrows at him sarcastically but he didn't look up. Mom was absorbed in the magazine rack across from us, having finally settled on a coffee mug and fridge magnets to bring to Nan.

I watched her pull a disgusted face as she flipped the page in *Star News Daily* before reaching for a glossy interior design mag. Not for the first time, I felt a familiar clash in my chest at the reality of our situation—we were all going to Ireland.

Together.

Of course, it was just for a visit. Leith and I only agreed to visit Nan once boundaries and terms had been laid out with no room for verbal, magical trickery. We would be returning to Boston after a week in the Irish countryside, return tickets and rides to the airport already booked and negotiated.

Mom hadn't decided whether she'd be coming back with us or not.

"I told you I'd take you," Leith said, finally looking up from his book.

"In your mouth," I said, smacking him playfully on the shoulder.

He pretended to be insulted. He'd offered to swim to Ireland, with me in my leprechaun form using his mouth as a carriage.

"It's a perfectly legitimate way to travel for a lady such as yourself."

"I don't want to ride in your wet mouth for twelve hours."

His eyes darkened and a half-smile crept up his face, but I put a hand to his mouth as my mom walked back up to us.

"Any luck?" I asked.

"More than enough to ensure we never miss a connection or a bag," she said and sighed. "But no magic in this realm or any other is enough to find a gift that will please your Nan."

"What did you find?"

Mom held up the coffee mug, which was neon green and had "Wicked Pisser" written on it in swirling font. She held up the magnets in the other hand, a trio of Boston landmarks etched tastefully in bronze.

I laughed and shrugged, sipping my coffee. "Well, she's gotta like one of 'em at least."

"She'll hate them," Mom said, tucking the gifts in her purse. "But I'd rather expect her distaste than fool myself."

"You're the real gift anyway," Leith said, nodding to my mom. She grinned at him, somewhat shy. They had yet to forge a real friendship after their initial tense encounter.

But I had hope for our trip together.

"Ladies and gentlemen, thank you for joining us on our non-stop flight to Dublin this afternoon" came from the microphone directly behind us.

"That's us," Mom said and stood, eyeing the line as it slowly built by the doors.

"You ready?" Leith asked, closing his book.

"Not even a little bit," I said, standing and sliding my hand into his. "But let's do it anyway."

Acknowledgments

No one writes a book in a vacuum and this wild little number is no exception. I owe huge thank yous to all my early and advanced copy readers who tolerated massive typos and weird autocorrect swaps. Thanks to Ashley and Guramar especially, your feedback helped me tighten the story into its best self. Thanks, kisses, love to Amber, my biggest fan for life and romance inspiration. Thank you for helping me brainstorm this story on your couch that summer. Finally, huge, endless thanks to my husband for supporting my dream of writing smutty romance novels in every way possible, and for dragging me to the National Leprechaun Museum which inspired the bawdier parts of this story.

About the Author

Kel Bruem proudly writes kissing books set in fantasy and science-fiction worlds. Her Kindle Vella series SNAPPED and BOLD DAMAGES are available and complete. WHAT'S LUCK GOT TO DO WITH IT is her debut romance novel, with a sequel forthcoming in Fall 2023.

You can connect with me on:
🌐 https://www.tiktok.com/@kelbruem

Subscribe to my newsletter:
✉ https://subscribepage.io/Iq43sX